Along the margin-sand

Cover design by
Nina Patel

Books by Peter Larner

Farewell Bright Star

Lost in a hurricane   *(Jack Daly Mystery 1)*

Deathbed Confessions   *(Jack Daly Mystery 2)*

The Unfolding Path   *(Jack Daly Mystery 3)*

The Jack Daly Trilogy   *(Compilation)*

Covenant of Silence   *(Covenant Conspiracy 1)*

Covenant of Retribution   *(Covenant Conspiracy 2)*

The Covenant Chronicles   *(Compilation)*

Harpoon Force   *(Jack Daly Mystery 4)*

One Christmas Past

Deathbed Betrayal   *(Jack Daly Mystery 5)*

Along the margin-sand

Sure Uncertainty

To my brothers

**John, Mike
and the little bloke**

*Truth is stranger than fiction, because fiction is obliged to
stick to possibilities and truth isn't.* - Mark Twain

Along the margin-sand

Peter Larner

1

The truth has been conspicuously absent from my life over these past few weeks. My mum is never forthcoming, even at the best of times, and these have not been the best of times. If only I could get her to swear an oath, because that seems to work for Perry Mason.

It would be inflammatory to describe her explanations as lies, but honesty is much more than simply not telling a lie. In my view, suppressing the truth is no different to lying, as one is simply the shadow of the other. I wish mum would be less reticent about sharing things with me. Soon I'll be a teenager, an adult, someone she can lean on, but she still sees me as a child, so that isn't going to happen anytime soon.

Uncovering the truth is what Perry Mason is good at and I intend to follow his example. The truth should never be hidden by secrecy or silence; honesty is not a private matter, it should never be hidden away or kept to ourselves.

I was aroused from my absentminded meanderings by a loud crashing sound. My mother had nodded off and was startled from her sleep, grabbing my arm tightly, until she realised it was only the noise of the truck as it disembarked from the ferry.

The ramp clattered loudly as the removal lorry rumbled down, off the ferry and on towards the exit from the harbour. Mum and I sat in a cramped rear seat behind the driver and the two other men who helped to load up our furniture. The rain that accompanied our journey across the Channel did not relent when we arrived in France. Somehow, I expected it to be much hotter in a foreign land, though I'm not sure why, because we had only driven for a few hours.

I was beginning to get pins and needles in my left foot, which was partly trapped by the metal frame of the passenger seat in front of me. I wriggled my toes in time with the windscreen wipers that thrashed at the rain and the tingling stopped.

My stomach was still recovering from the Channel crossing and any queasiness that remained was not improved by us driving on the wrong side of the road. I was not looking forward to life at our new home but, at this moment in time, it would be a big improvement on the rocking and rolling of the truck.

The men spoke quietly and the further we drove, the more I appeared to be living in a little piece of England that was trundling through a rain-swept foreign land. Everything looked different in France, but the conversation in the front seat was still about the test match, and of Roy Emerson's jittery service and how that Brazilian girl had remarkably beaten the number one seed Margaret Court at Wimbledon.

"Court beat her in Paris a few weeks ago, quite easily," the knowledgeable driver told his colleagues. I tried to ignore them, because if they weren't going to ask my opinion, then there was no point in listening to the conversation.

"Was Dad going to come with us?"

It seemed odd using the word 'dad' in the past tense. One of the men thought I was talking to him and turned around to look at me. I smiled and he turned back.

"Of course," my mum replied.

"Did he get a passport like us?"

"He'd ordered one," she answered a little too cautiously, which made me wonder whether I had received an honest reply.

I sensed that the men were listening to our conversation, so I returned to my comic. Alf Tupper had arrived late for the athletics meeting and the starter's pistol went off while he was still putting his running shoes on. It didn't seem important now. Anyway, I knew he would catch up with them. So I left the comic open and thought about my life being turned upside down. It felt like the gun had gone off and the world had left without me. I wasn't sure how I was going to catch up, but knew that I would get there, just like Alf Tupper always did.

Presumably, if my father had not died, I would have been called Little Peter until he had, or at least until he took on the byname of 'old Pete', and I became young Peter. Strangely, I would still have been Little Peter when I was taller than my father, who was simply Pete and was only ever referred to as 'big Pete' on special occasions, such as my birthday, when I gained some degree of antecedence. What is the statute of limitations for calling someone little, or junior, or young Peter? And is the statute of limitations trumped by the death of the aforementioned big, senior or old Pete? I never regarded 'Little Peter' as a term of endearment, but that is what my mother called it whenever I objected. 'Objection overruled', my dismissive mother would reply. I should never have told her that I wanted to be a lawyer when I grew up.

It stopped raining and in the distance there was a bright horizon waiting for us to drive straight into it. I hoped we didn't need to turn off before we got there.

The purpose of giving someone a name is, after all, in order to enable us to identify an individual, so why give a child the same name as his father to begin with? It rather defeats the object. Dad avoided confusion with constant references to me as 'the little bloke', which is no better, and indeed probably worse, than Little Peter. "Where's the little bloke?" he would ask Mum, when he arrived home from work. Objection your honour, the question is demeaning and defamatory.

I learned quite a lot about the law from TV programmes like Perry Mason and Burke's Law. Perry would object to any statement that the prosecution counsel made. In one episode he said: "Objection your honour, the question is incompetent, irrelevant and immaterial." Incompetent? That isn't a basis for an objection. Then there was Gene Barry, an entirely different character from Perry. For its part, Burke's Law demonstrated just how much money you can make as a lawyer; after all, he drove around in a Rolls Royce.

Mum could not speak French, which was just one of the mysteries surrounding our move to France. We had never been there on holiday, we couldn't speak the language, I had never eaten French food and nor had my mother as far as I know. So why were we emigrating to France? I had asked her, of course. She just said 'it's lovely there', or 'you'll really enjoy it'. But she never actually provided an answer. She was pretty good at not providing answers. When my questions about the move really got too much for her, she switched the subject completely. 'Perhaps we can get a dog', she would say, knowing how I had always wanted one, but Dad would never agree. Now she couldn't use that excuse, and it was difficult for her to counter my occasional requests for a pet. 'Your dad wouldn't like this, or your dad wouldn't like that,' was not a viable line of defence for Mum anymore. Now she would have to reject any ideas I had, or find a way of distracting me as she usually did.

When your father dies, a torrent of questions come into your head; firstly about your own and, more immediately, your mother's mortality, for she is responsible for feeding you and a slow death of hunger is much worse than a sudden one and I wasn't very confident of surviving without my mum.

What was that line in *The Importance of being Earnest*? It was either Edith Evans or Margaret Rutherford, I can never remember. 'To lose one parent may be regarded as a misfortune, but to lose both looks like carelessness.'

And then, after those two elements have been discharged, your own mortality and your mother's, you start to think of all the things you forgot to ask your dad when he was alive. Like what did he do in the war, or what did he do for a living? And I should have asked him what his parents were like, because I only ever met one set of grandparents? Or, perhaps, why did I not have any brothers or sisters? Because an older sister would certainly have been useful on a number of occasions, particularly now, and a younger brother would probably relieve me of the 'little' tag. It would have been quite difficult for family members to refer to me as Little Peter, if I was bigger than my younger brother, which I am sure would have been the case. But it was too late to ask any questions now. Now, I was left only with a mother to ask questions of, and she wasn't great at answering questions.

My dad had worked away from home for a couple of years. He should have been eager to talk about his time in Spain but he never spoke of it until I questioned him about it one Sunday, as we sat eating apple pie and custard, just before Robin Hood came on the TV. Even then, he just said it was okay. He was a man of fewer words than my mother. I'm not sure he could have enjoyed it that much, as he certainly didn't come home with a suntan as I imagined he would.

Dad had a reservoir of optimistic and encouraging expressions that he called upon to lift our spirits. 'Keep your chin up,' 'when life gives you lemons, make lemonade,' and 'it only takes a minute to score a goal'; the last of these is the sort of remark you tend to lean on a lot when you are a Hammers' fan.

The episodes of Perry Mason all had titles like, the case of the lawful Lazarus, or the case of the floating stones. So, whenever I was faced with something I couldn't understand, I would give it a name like that. The case of the mysterious Spanish trip was still listed as unsolved. It was no use asking Dad as he still thought I was too young to be consulted on anything, and asking Mum was a complete waste of time too.

My mother always told me what I wanted to hear, or rather, what she thought I wanted to hear. This is not the same as telling a lie she pleaded in her defence, it is just another version of the truth. Another version of the truth? Even the great Perry Mason would have trouble getting that one past his honour Judge Redmond.

If the truth is withheld, or another version of it takes its place, then it is almost as if the thing didn't exist, or the event didn't happen, and that isn't right. The truth must be remembered, for we do the past a disservice by ignoring it or replacing it with a falsehood.

The explanation she gave me for having to change our name sounded very much like another version of the truth. According to my mum, when your husband dies, the wife, or widow as she is now referred to, reverts to her maiden name. So Susan Longhurst became Susan Jackson and as a consequence, I became Peter Jackson. I had never heard of this particular law before, but I did not object, because this ridiculous suggestion she had concocted had at least two advantages that I could see. Firstly, I would not be referred to as little Peter anymore, because there wasn't a big Peter Jackson, only a lately deceased Pete Longhurst. And, secondly, my friends at school would have to stop calling me 'Martha', which I have to say is even worse than 'Little

Peter'. Although now, I didn't need to worry about that anymore, because my name was no longer Longhurst and I was living in France, where people had never heard of *Coronation Street* or its whinging old maid, Martha Longhurst.

The case of the changing name was a complicated one, because my mother never answered questions honestly. If she had been on the stand, I could have accused her of perjury, but she hadn't taken the oath. After due consideration, I decided not to launch an appeal in lieu of the two advantages I had gained if this other version of the truth was adopted.

I never went to my father's funeral. Mother said it would be too traumatic for me. In death, my dad became Big Pete and I became just Peter. Conversations hereafter will refer to 'when big Pete was alive' or, more likely, 'when my husband was alive' or even 'when my dad was alive', because nobody in Berck sur Mer knew my father, so it would only add to the confusion if we started referring to him as Pete.

The windscreen wipers made a scraping sound as they dispersed the droplets of rain that splashed up from the bonnet of the truck. The rain had stopped and the feint lines of a rainbow began to appear off to our left.

For the last two weeks, I had been a little preoccupied with the case of the magic powers. Rightly or wrongly, I had reached the conclusion that I had developed magic powers and had actually caused the deaths of two people as a consequence. Be careful what you wish for, people say, and they are right.

When I blew the candles out on my last birthday cake, I wished that something might happen to Martha Longhurst in order that I might not be subjected to being called Martha by the kids at school. Then, a few weeks later, the storyline changed and the character was going to leave the series and go to Spain. Phew! What a stroke of luck. But then, the poor woman suffered a heart attack and died.

What was it Len Fairclough used to say about her? She always looked as though she had lost a quid and found a ha'penny. That summed it up for me. The poor woman had died because I wished it to be so. The only compensation was that she was only a character in a TV series and I hadn't actually caused the death of a real person. When Dad died, I racked my mind, trying to remember if I had ever wished that something bad might happen to him. Thankfully, I couldn't recall such an event, although it was possible I may have said something when he left home a few years ago.

To be honest, I didn't know my dad very well, which sounds a strange thing for any son to say, but then he did go missing for those two years of my life. He only came back home just before my eleventh birthday, so I hardly had time or reason to wish him any harm. Mum said he had been working abroad and when I asked him, that's when he told me he had been in Spain.

There was another coincidence in the case of the magic powers, which is probably irrelevant. Martha Longhurst had just received her first passport, in order that she could travel to Spain. And, presumably my dad had just received his passport too, as he must have been planning to join us in France, although, there was never any mention of moving to

France until that manic Monday, two weeks ago. Dad had gone missing and granddad came to pick us up in his car and we went back to my grandparents' house, where I played endless games of Ludo with granny, whilst granddad and Mum whispered for hours in the living room. Given more time, I could have taken some of my board games from home, although granny wasn't great at complicated ones like Cleudo and Monopoly and all they have in their house are games like Ludo and Snakes and Ladders.

Two weeks later and without any consultation with me, the removal men were putting our furniture into the back of a truck and Mum and I were off to live in France. Before we left my grandparents house, I was told the sad news that my father had passed away the previous week and that was what all the mystery had been about. It was granny, of course, who was charged with telling me the sad news. Mum presumably knew that if she had been given the task, I might have asked more questions, but they knew I wouldn't embarrass granny by quizzing her about the details of his illness.

We approached a roundabout and the lorry lurched forward as the driver crunched the large gear stick back towards my right knee. I shut my eyes as we went around the circular island in the wrong direction.

"So, did Dad not already have a passport from when he worked in Spain?" I asked Mum when I opened my eyes again.

"It had expired."

2

About an hour after leaving the ferry point, the lorry passed a sign that said *Berck sur Mer*. One of the crew members rummaged about in his jacket pockets, withdrew a piece of paper, and began reading directions to the driver. He nearly missed a right-hand turn and I thought, for a moment, that he was going to head off down the wrong side of the road, which is the right side of the road in France.

All the vehicles on the road had strange looking number plates. Twenty minutes went by and the feeling that we were driving deeper and deeper into a foreign land grew in my stomach. The bumpy ride, the swaying of the truck and the loud engine noise was already having an effect on that part of my anatomy.

To distract myself, I needed a puzzle, a riddle, to occupy my mind, to take my mind off the lurching of the vehicle and the turmoil in my belly. Trying to solve what had happened to Dad wasn't going to help settle my insides, so I chose a broader subject. What were we doing here? What was my mum thinking of, taking us off to a foreign land? It probably wasn't a good idea to make important decisions, certainly not life-changing decisions, whilst you were still trying to get over the death of your husband.

When I was told we were moving to Berck, I assumed the spelling would be Burke, as in the TV programme Burke's Law, but I suppose Berck is the French spelling.

Eventually we arrived on the outskirts of a town and the driver turned on to smaller and smaller roads until we arrived in a narrow backstreet, the Rue des Fréres Minimes.

We parked outside an old, dilapidated house that spread itself along a lengthy stretch of the street. It seemed a little too big for just the two of us. There were no net curtains in some of the windows and the pale green paint of the building was flaking and exposing the crumbling brickwork beneath.

The crew members clambered out of the lorry and one of them helped my mother to exit, as gracefully as was possible, from the high cab of the vehicle. She told me to stay where I was until she had gained access to the building.

There were puddles, some of them quite deep, along the length of the road and Mum had to tiptoe around them to avoid splashing the rainwater up her legs.

The front door opened before she arrived at the top of the steps and a tall, but slightly built old man stood before her. He had obviously been waiting for us to arrive. I couldn't hear what was being said, but mother seemed entirely able to understand the man, even though he must have been speaking in French, after all, we were in France.

They stopped talking for a moment and then both looked up and down the road as if they were expecting someone. The man removed a fob watch from his waistcoat and raised it closer to his eyes. Another, shorter man, carrying a small attaché case came hurriedly around the far corner of the street and rushed towards the house. Mother waved to me and one of the men helped me climb down from the cab of the lorry.

Mother stepped forward to meet the almost smartly dressed man with the attaché case, who had become a little dishevelled in his rush, and they exchanged greetings. From a distance, he looked quite elegant in his three-piece suit but, on closer examination, you could see the frayed cuffs and re-sewn pocket.

"Bonjour," I said to the old man at the top of the steps, "Good afternoon," the man replied to me in perfect English.

He held his hand out and I climbed the steps to shake it. I like it when adults treated you as something more than just a blubbering child.

"I am Captain Trevelyan," the man told me. "I live on the first floor."

He released my hand and looked up towards the roof of the building.

"Von Tench lives in the attic."

I nodded and smiled, as if I was supposed to know who, or what he was talking about. With any luck it would be a dog or a parrot.

Mother was making less progress with the man who the Captain identified to me as 'the agent'.

He didn't look like any of the agents I had seen on TV. He was short, balding, with glasses and his threadbare suit.

"Bonjour Madame. Comment allez vous."

"Parlay voo Onglay," mother replied.

"A little," he answered, to her obvious relief.

The man then led the two of us into the house and showed us around the rooms. His voice echoed around the large, empty spaces.

The removal men began unloading the furniture and placing it in the rooms in the basement and at the back of the ground floor. But nothing was placed in the large room at the front of the ground floor, which had a wide bay window looking out onto the street. It was a large building, with high ceilings and a feint smell of mothballs. Who was going to climb up there to hang the Christmas decorations, I wondered to myself? But then I hoped we might not still be here in six months time.

The furniture clattered against the stone-tiled flooring in the hallway as the removal men made their way through the building with the chairs and table we had brought from England. We would have had little difficulty fitting all our belongings into just one of the very large rooms.

When she found the box containing the kettle, and after Captain Trevelyan had retrieved an adaptor from a box of junk on his landing, mother made everyone a cup of tea. The tea was followed by a less than stealthily delivered gratuity to the lorry driver and a wave goodbye, before the men set off in the lorry, back towards the port. My stomach had stopped tumbling around and I wandered around, following my mum into each room to examine it.

"At least it wasn't raining when they were unloading our furniture," Mum said as she gazed around at the higgledy-piggledy way the furniture had been arranged in our living room, which was in the basement, but still quite light.

It was only then that I noticed the absence of a television set and my heart sunk.

"It was a rental TV," Mum told me. "And it would be of no use in France, as all the programmes would be in a foreign language."

"So, just the radio then?"

"Not much point with that either," she replied. "I gave it to one of our old neighbours."

With my mind imagining countless dull evenings playing Ludo, which mother seemed to think required a degree of skill, I then began unpacking my belongings whilst she went upstairs with the Captain to meet the other tenant, Ludwig von Tench, who sounded distinctly German to me. A strange, pulsating noise came from the top floor, a contraption whirred loudly just like my grandmother's old sewing machine, only with a little more reverberation and clunking. It stopped when they reached the top floor and the three of them remained there for nearly an hour before Mum returned downstairs alone.

When she came back down, I pointed out to her that there did not appear to be a telephone.

"No," she replied. "The last owners didn't have one."

"Are we getting one?"

"When we have settled in."

"Because we'll need a telephone so that we can call granny and granddad."

She agreed, but seemed a little pre-occupied. After a few more cardboard boxes were emptied, Mum said that she needed to get something for our dinner that evening and I rather surprised her when I asked if I could go too.

Normally, I avoided shopping but, as the alternative was to stay in an eerie, old house with two equally curious old men, it wasn't particularly considerate of me. I also had the consolation that Mum was not going to bump into one of her friends, as she did on the way to Chrisp Street market, leaving me to stand around impatiently waiting for her to finish gossiping. I was also intrigued to find out how she was going to order the ingredients for our evening meal, as she spoke no French.

The Rue Carnot appeared to represent the high street, so we began our first expedition here. The baker was a man named Monsieur Fournier, who wished to be called Bruno. He spoke very good English and told us that his mother was originally from England, but had lived here for nearly fifty years. It was impossible to simply order a loaf of bread in France, because bread came in a variety of shapes and sizes. Mum just wanted a normal, sliced loaf.

"Wonderloaf," she declared loudly.

Bruno shook his head and recommended a long, stick-shaped loaf, but mother opted for one called a *boule*; and it was shaped a little bit like a ball, which made it easy to remember in case we wanted another one tomorrow. He then gave us directions to the butcher's shop and told us to tell Monsieur Dubois that Bruno had sent us. From this comment, we both assumed that Monsieur Dubois would be speaking English too. I was a little disappointed that my mum was not going to be severely tested and might even abandon the whole idea of moving to France simply because there was every chance that we would starve to death.

My disappointment was misplaced. Monsieur Dubois spoke only French, but he understood mother's explanation, in broken English, that Bruno had sent them. She pointed to the loaf of bread which she had just purchased.

"Beef," she said.

"Beouf," he replied and lifted up a piece of meat. "Pour deux." He pointed, alternately, at mother and me.

Beouf, I thought. This French language is much easier than I imagined.

Mother wasn't sure what the butcher meant, so he put the piece of beef down on the work surface in front of him and slammed a chopper into it. He lifted a small piece and mother nodded her head. He wrapped it up and she handed him a banknote. He said something in French and indicated that he wanted to see what other money she had. He smiled, took another note from her hand and returned the original one to her, with some coins.

Shopping at the greengrocer was much easier, for it consisted of simply pointing at things like potatoes and other vegetables and holding up fingers to indicate how much we wanted.

My mother seemed much relieved at having completed the first labour of Hercules by purchasing the ingredients for dinner in a foreign land. I was less impressed than my mother, as neither of us knew the French word for gravy, so the dinner would be a little dry. More disappointingly, we were probably weeks from learning how to say batter in French, so we wouldn't be enjoying Yorkshire puddings anytime soon.

That evening we sat in our new living room, without a TV or radio, and I was told what arrangements had been put in place for my education. Having just left my primary school and gained a place at a local secondary modern in Poplar, I was already prepared for some turmoil in my life. But, moving to another country put any domestic anxiety into context. What could be worse than joining a new school in September with, at best a smattering of the French language that I might have gained in the next six weeks? The answer to that question was what mother called 'home schooling'. My education, she explained, was being placed in the hands of the two peculiar old men who lived upstairs at the convent of the order of the little brothers. This last part of mother's description of my future schooling needed more explanation, for I had not realised we had entered a monastic order. She handed me a piece of paper showing details of the house she had just purchased.

Le Couvent l'ordres des Fréres Minimes was once home to an order of monks and subsequently housed Franciscan sisters, hence the confusing name of a convent for an order of monks. It was sold by the Catholic Church at the end of the Second World War, during which time it was occupied by the Nazis and used to house German officers. The 'for sale' document went to great lengths to explain that safe passage had been provided to the nuns who went off to Italy. The photograph of the building on the other side of the document made it look very much like the last outpost of the French Foreign Legion, rather than that of a long forgotten order of monks, and the building itself was made to appear even lonelier by its backstreet position away from the 'sandy shoreline of Berck sur Mer', as described in the pamphlet. If 'sur mer' meant 'by the sea', as was suggested, it was Berck-very-unsur-Mer, it seemed to me for I hadn't seen the sea since we drove off the ferry at Calais. The small, myrtle-walled courtyard at the rear of the property contains an ancient Yew tree, or so the caption read below a photograph of the rear of the property.

"Have we bought this house?" I asked nervously. "Because it says here that the cost is 65,000 francs."

"Do you know how much 65,000 francs is Peter?"

I shook my head but guessed it was an awful lot of money in any language. After all, the butcher had given us change from a one franc note for the joint of beef.

Home schooling meant that I would spend two mornings each week with Captain Trevelyan and two mornings with Mr von Tench. They would each give me work to do in the afternoon and, on Fridays, mother would attempt to teach me mathematics from a book that granddad had given her. Our two tenants had been offered a reduction in their rent if they agreed and the only difficulty they had with that decision was the division of their labour, because both wanted to teach history and geography. It was finally agreed that von Tench would teach French and history and the Captain would supervise my education in geography and the arts of English literature and language.

Very little information was ever offered voluntarily by my mother and, when it was, she was infuriatingly vague. Each element of my new life needed to be prised from her grasp. How did she suddenly come by such a substantial sum of money? Why have we emigrated to France? The answers to these questions were not released from her tight grip, but others were, like why are we not using the large bedroom at the front of the building?

Apparently, the house came with two long-term tenants and a spare room, suitable for short-term lets, such as holidaymakers wishing to take advantage of the sea air. That statement suggested that we were not far from the sea. Having seen Calais when we arrived on the truck, I didn't hold much hope that it was going to be anything like last year's summer holiday at Cromer.

3

My granddad would refer to unusual people as eccentric or, sometimes, bohemian. But, to granddad, that included anyone who did not wear a starched collar and cufflinks. My dad called them beatniks in a rather derogatory tone, but my mum never spoke ill of anyone, not even when she used to meet gossiping neighbours in Chrisp Street market. Von Tench and Captain Trevelyan were neither bohemian, nor eccentric; and they could certainly not be described as beatniks. My grandmother would have called them uncommonly quaint. And they were clearly extraordinary characters, with personalities that I had not seen the like of before.

Trevelyan was tall and very upright for an old man. He wore a tweed suit with a waistcoat, even when the weather demanded something much cooler. My impression was that this might have been the only suit he owned, as I am not sure he would have worn this by choice if there was another, because he was a proud man at heart. He had a fob watch in one pocket of the waistcoat, with a chain that drooped across to the other pocket. He had a generous head of grey hair for someone of his age and he was clean shaved except for a thin moustache that I guessed was an attempt to look like Errol Flynn or Ronald Colman.

My mother liked Ronald Colman very much and one of my oldest memories is how she cried when she learned of his death. It seemed strange to cry over someone you had never met and he was an actor anyway, so it was probably the character he played in Random Harvest that she was crying about, not Ronald Colman himself. My mother didn't cry easily, which is why the memory had stayed with me, I suppose.

Ludwig von Tench, who lived in the attic, was shorter than the Captain, with much less hair, just two patches, in fact, of waxy black strands separated by a parting that was bigger than both the patches added together. Unlike Trevelyan, he wore glasses, although I think the Captain needed them too. Ludwig's were small, half-rimmed spectacles which he perched upon his nose and peered above them at the world. He had a moustache too, but this was bushier than the Captain's and had nearly as much growth as the hair on top of his head. He looked a bit like Clement Atlee, or at least as much like him as Trevelyan looked like Ronald Colman.

Not that I would have known who Clement Atlee was, if it wasn't for my friend Terry Williams, who lived in a block of flats in Poplar that had been named after the politician. In the lobby area of these flats there was a picture of Atlee hanging on the wall opposite the lift, protected by reinforced glass to stop boys like us drawing on it. There wasn't any need for the protective glass anyway, because he already had a moustache and wore glasses. The worse we could have done was to give him a full head of hair and this would have just made him look more presentable.

Terry Williams, number 3, Clement Atlee House. He must wonder what happened to me because he was on holiday at Butlin's Holiday Camp when the decision to move to France was made. Knowing Terry, I imagine he has told everyone we were abducted by aliens.

I asked my mum about writing to Terry, to let him know where I was. She agreed, but suggested we leave it a few weeks, so that I had something to tell him.

"I've got something to tell him," I declared. "We've emigrated to a foreign land."

"This isn't a foreign land, Peter," she answered, "it's France."

Trevelyan walked with a limp, favouring his left leg, and I assumed this was an injury from the war; after all he was a former British Army captain.

The rent reduction which mother offered them applied with immediate effect, which was good news for the unlikely allies who lived upstairs, but bad news for me, because the six-week summer holidays did not apply to home-schooling according to my mum.

"Why?" I asked, not expecting to receive a sensible answer. I wasn't disappointed.

"It's just the way it is in France."

I fancied that this statement was destined to become a stock expression in my new life. It was my job, in 'the case of the lame excuse', to disprove as many of these other versions of the truth as I could.

I reported to Captain Trevelyan's billet, as he called it, straight after breakfast the following morning. It was a hideous room containing a ragged old armchair, a sideboard, dark, heavy curtains, which had the thickness of a rug and, in one corner, there sat a radio with a scratchy reception playing classical music, the news and the shipping forecast on the BBC.

On their own, neither the furnishings nor the scratchy radio made the room hideous. That was achieved without the aid of furniture, for the living room walls formed a palisade of books, from floor to ceiling on every wall. Only the window, that looked out on the myrtle-walled courtyard was unencumbered by books of every kind, none of which seemed to be in any particular order to my untrained eye.

I could sense that the Captain wanted to say something, but he kept his silence and seemed to garner some deep pleasure from my eye-boggling journey around his parlour. I had visited a library before but this was far more intense, as if the books hovered over the entire room and every piece of information you would ever want to know was secured there, rammed tight against the wall of this room. How on earth did he gather such a collection and had he read them all? Eventually he spoke, yet more to himself than me.

"Now, where to start?" he asked himself as he showed me to his writing desk, where I was to sit for the lesson. "Poetry or a novel?" We were obviously beginning with English, rather than geography.

He decided on poetry and walked over to a section of his library on the far wall.

"Shelley, Byron," he commented to himself as he fingered the books along the shelf without removing them. "Keats is the greatest of the Romantic poets," he mumbled as if it was a fact and not just an opinion that he foisted on anyone who would listen.

"If Keats is the greatest, isn't that the best place to begin?" I asked.

"If we begin with the best, where will we go from there?"

He looked at me for some contribution to our stubby little conversation and asked if I knew any English poets. He had clearly dismissed the idea of any other nationality, which was a relief, bearing in mind that we were living in France now.

"Wordsworth," I replied, naming the only poet I knew and hoping, beyond hope, that I would not be summoned to recite something from memory. 'I wandered lonely as a cloud that floats on high and then another line ending in crowd', I thought to myself. Please don't ask me, I hoped, contemplating the worse. But the embarrassing challenge never materialised.

"What respectable poet would have his wife as a muse?" he answered rhetorically.

I wanted to ask what a muse was, but he was still mumbling his reproval of my suggestion.

"Lyrical Ballads," he snarled, as if my words had offended his very soul. "And yet," he mumbled under his breath, as he walked over to a shelf near the corner of the room. "Barrack Room Ballads," he said and handed me a book of poems by Rudyard Kipling. "This is where you shall begin your education."

I wanted to tell him that I had already been attending school for about eight years but decided to keep my own counsel on the matter.

I wondered how he knew exactly where to find the book he required, for it was just one of so many in the rather disparate array of printed works. These books are not in alphabetical order, I wanted to tell him. And yet, you managed to find the one you wanted immediately, but I thought about it and decided it was a magic trick, created to impress me, so I remained silent.

But he read my mind and knew exactly what I was thinking.

"They are in a very specific order," he told me and then quickly changed the subject before he had to disclose the age-old secret of his shelving arrangement. "What did your father do?" he asked.

I looked at him with a vague expression, not sure of what his question meant.

"He died."

"No, I mean, what was his employment? What did your father work at?"

I noted that he didn't attempt to say he was sorry to learn about my father's death, like everyone else did when I told them. The Captain struck me as an impatient individual, restless to move the conversation on and not one who could be accused of being over sentimental. Almost everyone I met, which hadn't been too many people since I was told of my father's passing had said they were sorry for my loss. I never understood that. What were they apologising for? They hadn't been responsible for his death. It was just what people said, I told myself.

"I don't know."

"You don't know. Did you never ask your mother what your father did for a living?"

"My mum isn't very good at answering questions."

He gave me a withering look.

"Then I sincerely hope you do not take after her."

The remark made it clear that the Captain was not going to tip-toe around me, just because I had lost my father at a very young age.

I really didn't know what my father's job was. And, because he often worked away from home, my dad seemed to wander in and out of my life. He provided parenting by instalments. There were long periods when he was at home, like any normal dad, but these were interspersed with frequent intervals of absence, some for months and once, that time when he went to Spain for a couple of years.

Mum did not work, although I suppose there must have been a time when she did, before I was born probably. Surely nobody goes directly from school to being a housewife, but she never spoke of having a job, just about wanting one or, more correctly, the independence a job would have given her. I know she wanted to work and I can remember listening to conversations between my parents on the subject from time to time. Mostly, Mum would tell my dad that she fancied doing something to occupy her time, or earn a little bit of pocket money for herself, instead of relying on him to provide all the money she ever needed. And, every so often, she would tell Dad over dinner that there was a part-time job at the fish shop, or working in the shoe shop at Chrisp Street market, but he always found an excuse to prevent her applying. 'You won't qualify for any holiday entitlement for a whole year,' he would say, 'so we won't be able to go to Cromer.' There was always some reason why Mum should not get a job, just as there was always some reason why Dad had to go away to work for a few weeks, or longer.

As a family, we seemed to come in and out of money at irregular intervals. Sometimes it was a quarter of Merry Maids and other times it was just a penny bag of broken biscuits. And, when times got really hard, I would mix some cocoa powder and sugar together and dip my licked finger in it. These were the same times that dripping or margarine replaced butter. Maybe I didn't notice the reason for these fluctuations, as it was probably the result of Dad working away, because surely he would have earned much better pay for doing a job that kept him away from home for months on end.

Often, when Dad was working away and particularly when he was in Spain for two years, money was tight. And other times, it was the opposite. I had lots of toy cars and at Christmas, two years ago, I was given a massive Silverstone race track with dozens of Corgi racing cars. I guess my parents knew by then that I didn't believe in Father Christmas anymore, because the track had been set up in the living room when I got up in the morning. Father Christmas is a generous man, but he certainly wouldn't have time to set the toys up in every household he visited. I received a Waddington game as a present every Christmas, so I ended up with quite a lot of them. Not just Monopoly and Cleudo, but Totopoly, Formula 1, Careers and Scoop. I think the games influenced me as much as the TV programmes I loved.

So, during my early childhood, I wanted to be a racing driver, a journalist and, of course, a detective. Whenever I visited my grandparents, I always took a game with me. I brought the games with me to France, but I can't imagine playing with them again, as there is only me and Mum now, and she finds Ludo challenging.

The English lesson was quite interesting, in spite of Trevelyan having no teaching experience, or none that I knew of. He said he needed to find out what level I was at before he could decide on a programme of lessons. There was a noisy old clock on the mantelpiece of the small fireplace and I guessed he would let me finish by twelve o'clock, because Mum must have told him that we always have lunch at that time.

Captain Trevelyan ignored the clock and looked at his fob watch before deciding the lesson was over. My homework was to read at least ten of the poems in the book and memorise one of them. I was also to write a description of the house in which I now lived. He did not call it an essay and I wondered whether he wanted a description by way of size and layout or, quite the opposite, a description of the house and the strange people it provided shelter for.

The lesson ended at lunchtime, as abruptly as it began. I had the afternoon to complete my homework although, with no temporary guests in residence yet, I was at least able to use the much vaunted and currently unoccupied myrtle-walled courtyard for that purpose.

4

As I had not been introduced to our other tenant, Ludwig von Tench, my journey up the stairs to the attic the following morning was like the steps up to the gallows. I had seen him, peering over the landing on the day we moved in, but he made no attempt to meet us, as Captain Trevelyan had done.

All I kept thinking to myself, as I clumped my way up the stairs in order to let him know I was coming, is that we had a German living in our attic; one who spent most of his time carving out jigsaw puzzles on an old scroll saw that sat upon the landing outside his two rooms. It seemed a strange proposition and something I would not have imagined happening a couple of weeks ago.

I paused on the final step and examined the saw. It did look like an old sewing machine, but with a narrow saw instead of a needle. Just like granny's Singer, there was a large pedal at floor level but, instead of a wheel to turn, it had an array of horizontal and vertical levers. I was still trying to see how it worked when a voice spoke behind me.

"It's a pedal-powered treadle saw. I use it for making wooden jigsaws."

The rather solemn looking gentleman turned out to be a genial character, more approachable and less intense than the Captain. He looked slightly older, but it was probably his lack of hair that made him look so. He wore cavalry twill trousers and a corduroy jacket. The absence of a waistcoat made his appearance less formal, almost like the only male teacher at my primary school. He wasn't wearing a jacket when he looked over the landing the other day, so I guess he had put it on to make an impression, to ensure the proceedings had a more formal aspect.

I wasted no time in explaining the urgency around communicating with the local shopkeepers and, whilst he seemed a little put out at having his programme of lessons disturbed, he agreed that we could begin my first lesson with some written and spoken French. Mr von Tench spoke good English and French, as well as German of course, and three hours went by considerably quicker than the previous morning with Trevelyan. It wasn't that Trevelyan was a less interesting character, as much as the subject matter held my attention, as learning new subjects often does.

By the time I went downstairs for lunch, I had mastered some basic spoken French, including hello, goodbye, bread, milk, fish, beef, potatoes and I could count from one to ten.

"Bonjour, au revoir, s'il vous plaî, merci, un pain, un boutelle de lait, boeuf, pomme de terre, un, deux, trois, quatre, cinq, six, sept, huit, neuf, dix." I chanted to my mother as she prepared a sandwich for my lunch.

For my homework I had to write down, read out and memorise ten sentences, including 'puis-je avoir un boutelle de lait' and 'où est le médecin'.

"Where is the medicine?" mother laughed. "Where is the medicine?" she repeated, suggesting the expression was not something I needed to learn as a matter of urgency.

"No, where is the doctor," I corrected her.

"Let's hope we don't need one just yet, young man," she answered before giving me the job of buying a loaf of bread in the morning, so we could have toast with the marmalade she had brought with us from England.

"Puis-je avoir un pain, s'il vous plaî, Monsieur Bruno," I recited from memory when I arrived in the shop the next morning.

"Par fait, par fait," came the response I wanted to hear.

He wrapped the loaf and I handed him the coins I had been given.

"Can you do something for me?" he asked.

"Of course, if I can."

"I need to deliver a loaf of bread to my mother who lives near the beach, but I don't want to leave the shop unattended."

"Is there a beach?" I asked, wondering whether the French concept of a beach was anything like a British beach.

"Of course there is a beach."

"A sandy beach?"

"Of course," he answered with a suggestion that there was only one kind. He clearly had never been to Winchelsea. I had, for a weekend with Terry Williams and his parents, and every grain of sand that ever sat there had been replaced with harsh, sharp pebbles and stones that tore at the soles of your feet. The martyrs' beach, Mrs Williams called it, because crossing the beach for a swim required a sacrificial laceration of the feet before dunking your bloodied toes in the salty sea.

"Right then, I'll take it for you, Bruno, but I need to let my mother know where I am, or she will worry."

"That's fine."

I ran home as quickly as my feet would carry me and handed the loaf of bread over to my mother, before telling her about the errand I needed to run. She agreed, of course, and said she would have the toast ready for my return.

I hurried back to the bakers to collect the loaf and then set off, following the directions given to me by Bruno. I continued straight along the Rue Carnot until I could almost smell the sea air and feel the visualised sandy beach beneath my feet, then turned right along the promenade and looked for the next turning on the right, which is where Madame Fournier lived. I paused on the esplanade and looked up and down. In one direction, the narrow coast road stretched off into the distance, around a large bay and disappeared inland. The same road travelled only a small distance in the other direction before turning inland, in order to avoid the hilly sand dunes that blocked my view.

The beach itself was an enormous expanse of sand that spun out towards a distant ocean, not a stone, shell or piece of gravel in sight; eat your heart out Terry Williams, no martyrs' beach for me.

The white surf of the waves was so far away that it crashed silently on the shore. I was overcome by the desire to explore the beach, but needed to deliver the bread and get home for breakfast before lessons began.

Bruno's mother lived in the third house in the Rue de la Plage, the one with the green door. I was bursting with enthusiasm for my discovery when I met Madame Fournier. It was the widest, longest beach I had ever seen, I told her. It was so wide, that it was impossible to see the ocean. I had visited Southend-on-sea, but when the tide was out there, all you could see were mud banks and sad looking fishing boats exiled in a sea-less estuary. But here, the sand stretched out to the far horizon. I gave the old woman the loaf of bread and she thanked me.

I rushed home to tell my mum about what I had discovered. Although, it was hardly a discovery; it was just there, at the end of the road, waiting to be found.

"What about Madame Fournier?"

"Oh, she was lovely. I wasn't there very long, but she had a strange way about her."

Mother looked at me a little worryingly.

"She said I reminded her of her son, when he was a child. I think she misses people to talk to in her native tongue, because she talked to me like I was grown up."

I ate the toast and marmalade and Mum agreed that we should go to the beach on Sunday.

"Objection, your honour, what is wrong with Saturday?"

"Objection overruled, we have new guests arriving on Saturday."

"But the first ones only arrive today."

"Yes, Mr and Mrs Pearson are only here for two nights, but the Remilly family will be here for one week."

Mother handed me the red exercise book and pointed upwards as she opened the kitchen door.

"Captain Trevelyan awaits."

And he was waiting for me too. The Captain mumbled a good morning and took the exercise book from me, but did not open it. Instead, he asked me what I was reading at the moment. The *Victor* and the *Valiant*, I told him. He shook his head.

"Who is it by?"

"I'm not sure."

"What is it about?"

"*They*," I replied, "they contain lots of different stories, like Alf Tupper in *Tough of the Track* and Captain Hurricane in *The Steel Claw*."

"Short stories?"

"Comics, actually," I answered.

I suggested I fetch them, so he could examine them, which he did.

He flicked through the two comics and returned them to me, before asking what books I had read. I thought for a moment and recalled three books that I had been given for various birthdays and Christmas in recent years. *Black Beauty*, *Treasure Island*, and *The complete tales of Uncle Remus*. He smiled and said he considered these a good start. He invited me to choose a book from the many hundreds that lined the walls of the room and I immediately went to where he had replaced the poetry book he had given me to read. But the books didn't seem to be in any order that I could understand. There were quite a few by Kipling but, further along, I found a large book with a picture of a battle on the front cover. The men had spears and swords, rather than rifles and hand-grenades, so I pulled it out. It was much heavier than the poetry book I had read extracts from the previous afternoon.

"Herodotus?" He asked when I showed it to him. He seemed pleased, but said I might find a great number of words I didn't understand.

"I can ask."

"Yes, you must always ask," he replied and took the book from me. He flicked through the pages and placed a bookmark about halfway through the book. "Read this section for your homework. It tells the story of Leonidas, a great Greek warrior."

Whilst he read the entry in my exercise book, I recited *'Shillin' a day'* by Rudyard Kipling. I finished before the Captain did and stood there in silence for a few minutes, wondering if he knew I had come to the end of the poem, but he didn't look up, so I spoke.

"Some of Kipling's spelling is very poor, Captain."

He looked up.

"Like 'nervis' instead of nervous. And he drops a few aitches too," I added.

"It is written in the vernacular; it is meant to have been written and spoken by a common soldier."

"Whose name is O'Kelly," I replied.

He nodded.

"What does that mean?"

"What, the poem?"

"No, vernacular."

"It is the language spoken in the tongue of the ordinary people. He wrote poetry that way in order to reach a larger audience."

I nodded. "And he says gawd save the Queen," at the end.

"Quite." He stood up and retrieved another book from the shelf.

"He is a very good writer, Peter. He won the Nobel prize for literature."

"Well, presumably his spelling improved then."

The Captain ignored my attempt at wit.

"This isn't homework," he said, as he handed me a copy of *Kim* by Kipling. "Just read it in your own spare time."

I put it on top of the copy of Herodotus and he looked at me, then looked back at the exercise book on his lap.

"This seems to be less about the house than its tenants."

I told him that I was unsure what he wanted me to write about.

He ignored my response and commented that the spelling was very good, with just a few mistakes.

"Written in the vernacular," I answered and he looked at me for a moment before he realised I was being sarcastic. He smiled and asked me what a beatnik was.

"It's an expression my dad used. The only one I ever saw wore a beret and a roll neck sweater and played the bongos."

The Captain ignored my answer. "Some of what is written about the house," he finally said, looking at the contents of the exercise book, "is well described. I particularly like the expression *myrtle-walled courtyard*. And your research for the piece is very good. But, should you not explain why Le Couvent l'ordres des Fréres Minimes has such a confusing name?"

"It was once home to an order of monks and subsequently housed Franciscan sisters."

"Then you should have said so," he commented.

He complimented me on my knowledge of the building and thanked me for not considering him eccentric or bohemian.

"My mum suggested the word."

"Eccentric or bohemian?"

"Both, really."

A few moments later, that same mum arrived in the doorway to tell me that lunch was ready. She looked a little angry about something and she told me to go down to the kitchen as my sandwich was on the table. As I trudged slowly downstairs, I heard her ask the Captain not to play the radio whilst her son was having lessons, as he will find it distracting, she said, her voice was trembling a little. It seemed strange that she felt anxious about speaking with the Captain on such a mundane issue and he certainly did not take offence by it.

It was obvious, over lunch, that mother was upset about something and had taken it out on poor Captain Trevelyan for playing his radio during my lesson. But that was not the cause of her distress. Nor, I am sure, was it the fact that the sideboard had been moved, or some paperwork had mysteriously transported itself from the top drawer of that sideboard to a lower one. The blame for this fell to me, but I was less guilty than the Captain. I could have made a joke of it with a Perry Mason comment, but Mum was not in the mood for trivialities.

The following morning, I climbed back up the stairs to the attic, where von Tench was working on a jigsaw made from a picture of a desert scene, with soldiers from the French Foreign Legion. I was holding one of the books I had been given by the Captain, intending to return it to him, and Von Tench took this from me and examined it.

"Wait here," he instructed me, before stomping down the stairs to the floor below.

A row ensued. It was the responsibility of von Tench to teach history and the Captain to educate me in geography, declared the German. So why, he asked, had the boy been given a copy of Herodotus, a book tracing the *history* of the Greek-Persian war? The book is a classic of English literature, the Captain replied.

"You always have to interfere," blurted von Tench.

"That was not my intention Ludwig," said Trevelyan, who was now feeling extremely sorry for himself, having received two reprimands in as many days. For a moment, I thought he was going to cry, but he remained composed. Then something very odd happened. Von Tench wrapped his arms around the Captain and whispered in his ear. It reminded me of how Dad reacted when he had upset my mum, which was fairly often.

Von Tench appeared a little startled when he looked up the stairs and saw me gazing down. He had forgotten I was still there, waiting for my lesson.

"Give me back the Herodotus, Peter," the Captain said. "It is a little too advanced for you at the moment." Then he seemed to remember something. "I have something else for you," he said and went back into his room to retrieve it.

"It's an old journal, which the former owners used for visitor comments, back in the time when they had short term tenants. They left it with me but I think you should have it; you might want to let your guests start using it again."

I came down the stairs and took the journal from him. It looked like a large accounts book, but it contained only lines, not cash columns inside. Less than half of the journal had entries in, each one in a different handwriting. Those entries ended and the rest of the pages were blank.

"Thank you. Perhaps I'll get our guests to write stuff in it, about their holidays here."

The Captain smiled and went back into his room.

Von Tench and I returned upstairs and, not to be undone, he also declared that he had a gift for me. It was a jigsaw of the Eifel Tower.

"Thank you," I said and placed it on top of the journal by the door.

When the lesson ended, I took the journal into the garden and waited for Mum to finish making our sandwiches for lunch. I opened the book at the most recently completed page and flicked backwards from there. It hadn't been used since 1960 and that entry was in French. In fact, most of the entries were in French, although I did find some in English. In the main, the scribbling consisted largely of mundane comments about the weather, the guest's journey to Berck or about the food they ate. The previous owners had not written anything in the book, so it was impossible to determine who they were. I wondered why they had left the journal with Captain Trevelyan instead of just leaving it for us to find.

I turned over the pages until I found a comment in English. *'Took a long beach walk, over the dunes. Glorious weather for this time of year. Looking forward to the Beaujolais Noveau.'* It was dated November 1959. Earlier that year there was another entry I could read. *'Walked to the Town Hall and through the market. Had coffee in the Voltaire.'* I then found an observation about the house, or rather the garden. *'Pretty courtyard, perfect for relaxing, until we heard the history of the place.'* I read this sentence a couple of times and wondered whether they were referring to the house or to the town of Berck in general.

Back in 1957 there was a remark which was quite clearly written by a child. I think it said *'Perfect for flying my kite.'*

I went into the kitchen and showed Mum the journal that the Captain had given me. She flicked through it, as I did, stopping occasionally to read the entries which were written in English. She looked back a bit further than I did and found some more.

'Went to Montreuil and walked the ramparts, stunning views,' one entry said.

"That sounds nice," Mum commented. "Perhaps we could go to Montreuil, wherever that is."

"It is about eight miles away; the Captain told me as part of my geography lesson. It is where the British Army established their headquarters after D-day. I'm not sure how we would get there though."

Mum didn't take any notice and continued reading the English entries in the journal.

'Very nice room. Might go to the circus in town tomorrow. Mildred won the bridge tournament again.'

"Oh," murmured mother a little too enthusiastically. "There is a circus that comes to town. Or at least it did back in 1953."

"I'm going to put the journal in the hallway for our guests to write things in," I declared.

"That's nice," Mum replied.

"Not Captain Trevelyan and Mr von Tench, but the other short stay guests.

"That's probably best dear."

"I'll put a sign above it saying that guests are required to make a daily entry in the Visitors' Journal."

Mum looked at me a little sternly.

"I think the notice should say that guests are *invited* to make a daily entry in the Visitors' book," she said, as if she didn't actually think it, but required it.

And so it was. I wrote the sign and placed it above the journal, which rested on a small bookcase in the hall, directly opposite the door to the guests' room.

That night I lay in bed wondering whether there was any significance in the Captain wishing me to read a section of Herodotus and von Tench objecting to it. The great Greek leader Leonidas was betrayed; the traitor Ephialtes showed the Persians a small track, a coastal path that led through the mountains to a position behind the Greek lines. This was a battle of unimaginable proportions. Four thousand men, led by Leonidas and his three hundred Spartans held off an opposing army of three million people – almost the entire Persian nation who had crossed the Bosphorus and attacked at harvest time, in order that an army of such size could be fed. The only one who stood between them and victory was Leonidas, who held them at the pass until he was betrayed.

5

My mother was both a poor communicator and someone who was tortuously independent. I choose that word purposely, because it is a form of torture to be kept in the dark and I speak as someone who has suffered in this way. I always assumed it was something to do with my mum being an only child, but the same privileges did not extend to me, as her only child. I was expected to keep her informed of where I was going, when I would be back and every detail between my leaving and returning. I was never allowed, as she was, to simply disappear for an hour or two and was certainly not permitted to make impulsive decisions without consulting her. But mother did.

Perhaps she thought she had told me, because often she would look at me as if I should have known what her intentions had been, such as using our new front bedroom as a holiday let to supplement her income, or walking me out to the forest on the outskirts of town, near the old aerodrome, to buy a puppy, which is what happened once we had greeted our first guests.

Mr and Mrs Pearson were celebrating their tenth wedding anniversary and had left their two small children with their grandparents. It was just a two-night break, which suited mother, because she also had a booking for a

French family arriving on Saturday. The short, balding man, with glasses and a threadbare suit, who met us on our arrival here, was arranging the short term lets for mother, she had told me that much. He was the estate agent who arranged the purchase of the house and now he was responsible for letting the spare room. He had an office in town, which was probably where mother disappeared to from time to time.

Once Mum had shown the new guests all the facilities, as she called them, she went to get her coat, leaving me in the hallway. I explained to the Pearsons about the resurrected journal and they considered themselves greatly honoured to be the first guests at the convent and the first to make an entry in the journal for several years. Once the pair had unpacked and set off towards the beach, Mum and I were left alone and it was then that she told me about the surprise she had for me and took me off to buy the puppy. She suggested I put a proper pair of shoes on, as we were heading out to the forest, which seemed a funny place to buy a dog.

The kennels were situated on the edge of the wood, close to the town and on the road leading to an airfield which stood in a large clearing and was still used by smaller, private airplanes for it was certainly too small to accommodate any commercial aircraft.

Mother had learned about the dog from Bruno, who told her that the breeder had only one puppy left from a litter of five; all the others had been sold. It was a wired haired fox terrier, a breed which the woman apparently specialised in. The dog was a tiny bundle of curly white hair with brown ears and brown markings on the head and body, and a large black patch on its back.

The owner of the kennels said that I could name the puppy, if I wanted to, because it hadn't been given a name yet, just a pedigree name, which was far too complicated for a puppy to respond to.

"What is her pedigree name?" I asked.

The owner didn't know the English translation, but it was something not dissimilar to Normandy monarch of fortune. I agreed that this was a little too wordy for such a small creature.

"What do you think, Peter?" asked Mum.

"Well," I answered, "we're here in a wood and the puppy is like a little orphan, the last of the litter. So if it's a boy dog, we could call him Hansel and if it is a girl, she could be named Gretel."

"Gretel it is then," the woman said as she fixed a lead to the collar around the puppy's neck. "Gretel, the Normandy Queen of Fortune."

She handed me the lead and Gretel tugged at it fiercely, wanting us to run off together, into the dark wood. Once the dog had been paid for, mother and I took Gretel for her first walk, back to her new home. It took a little longer because Gretel insisted on sniffing at every tree and lamppost on the way.

I was given responsibility to walk the dog every morning and every evening, so the following morning, I took her on a walk up to the beach and then back down to the bakers to collect a fresh loaf of bread. She was a little breathless after such a long walk, especially as she wanted to pull me from one lamppost to another on the way.

Bruno said his mother would love to meet Gretel and suggested I call in there when I took the puppy for her walk that evening.

Every time Gretel arrived in new surroundings, she scampered here and there, sniffing and getting very excited. Mother insisted that Gretel was kept on a lead when visiting Madame Fournier and gave me a cream slice cake as a gift for the old woman. It seemed an entirely inappropriate gift, considering her family had been bakers for generations and we had purchased the cake in her family shop. The one thing she had a surplus of was probably bread and cakes and yet mother chose to give her one as a gift. Perry Mason stood up and objected to my appeal, even before I voiced it. There was a lack of jurisdiction, your honour. I looked at the cake and then back at mother. Keep silent, I decided, or you could find yourself in contempt of court. In the case of the Curious Bride, Perry advised his client to 'say nothing and plenty of it.' I followed his good advice.

Bruno's mother was named Veronica, the baker had told me, but everyone called her Veronique, because that is how they pronounce the name in France. Veronique lived alone in a small house which, in spite of having just two rooms downstairs, the parlour at the front of the building was rarely used. I surmised that this was because of the staleness that greeted us as we went into it. It smelled like moth balls, although it was pleasantly cool on such a hot evening. Veronique made us a pot of tea and cut the cream slice in half for us to share. I think I was supposed to be greatly honoured at being invited into the smelly parlour, but it didn't feel that special.

Madame Fournier turned out to be a very talkative woman, who did not get out much and probably didn't have very many visitors to her home. She told me that, in her youth, she had trained to be a nurse and worked at a famous hospital in London called Guy's. During the First World War, she came to France to work as a nurse, looking after British soldiers who had been injured in battle. She met her husband here when he was serving in the French army.

"He was in the Régiment du Matériel," she said and recognised the blank look on my face. "The quartermaster stores," she explained. "After all, he was a baker, he could cook and an army marches on its stomach."

After the war, they got married and continued to live in Berck, where her husband came from. She was born before the turn of the century, she told me. In times, so long past I calculated that the famous Wild West Marshall, Wyatt Earp was still alive, although she said she had never heard of him.

Veronique knew so much about a great number of things, especially when it came to Berck sur Mer having lived here for so many years. She was familiar with my new home, the convent building, and had obviously visited it in the past because she described several rooms and the small courtyard garden in great detail. She told me that the nuns at the convent would use the berries from the myrtle tree that covered all its walls, to make rosaries for their devotion. Once the white flowers of summer had died off and the purple berries took on a firmer, darker texture, they could be removed and threaded onto a piece of twine.

As she was talking, she got up and went into her bedroom to get something. She was gone a short time, so I wandered around her room, looking at a few faded black and white photographs she had in wooden frames on the sideboard. The people in the pictures all looked as if they had lived at the time of Wyatt Earp. I was sure that one of the young men in a photograph was Bruno. He was wearing short trousers and was about my age. He was standing between an older boy and a girl.

"The myrtle was held in great esteem in pagan times too," Veronique told me in a hushed voice as she returned to the room carrying a set of roughly made rosary beads, "Because it could be used to interpret the meaning of dreams."

She gave me the rosary to look at. It had five rows, each of ten purple berries, and each row was separated by a single pink berry taken from the myrtle before it they turned to the darker shade. The four pink beads, she told me, signify the four groups of mysteries. There are five joyful mysteries, five sorrowful mysteries, five glorious mysteries, and five luminous mysteries and each of these has five elements

Each rosary of berries, she said, was kept with the nuns always and they prayed tirelessly. The sound of their Latin chanting still echoes around that building she added and, with a croaky voice she tried to sing their sorrowful or joyful laments.

"In nomine Patris, et filii, et Spiritus Sancti. Amen."

She made the sign of the cross and beckoned me to come closer.

"Some of the nuns secreted a second rosary away, using a small purse or tiny jewellery box. These were for another, more arcane and time-worn purpose that the beads served; a pagan ritual from our ancient past. For the berry beads were taken out on the Eve of Saint Agnes or on the Eve of Saint Mark, in accordance with the ways of yore. On the first of these feast days, it was said that a young woman, a virgin," she added, looking at me to see whether I knew what the word meant. She noticed my raised eyebrows and continued. "A virgin who was hoping to marry would, if she obeyed the ordinance of the custom, dream of her loved one on the Eve of Saint Agnes and thereby see the person she would marry."

She repeated a similar tale of the second feast day, on which a vision could be beheld, by those who wished to know such things, of those parishioners who would pass from this life in the coming year. Such prophetic dreams, she told me, were only possible through the aid of the myrtle beads and only upon those particular nights.

"And nuns did such things?"

"Even the ancient Catholic faith has remnants of its pagan past."

I got up and went back over to the sideboard, to ask her if the smaller boy in the photograph was Bruno.

"Yes, that is Bruno." But she did not say who the two other, older children were and I chose not to ask.

Veronique told me about the Great War, the memories of which appeared too fresh to be true. And she spoke of her work as a nurse in the Second World War, which was less great, apparently, than the first one. She said again, that I reminded her of her son, when he was small. And then, without my prompting, she began talking about Captain Trevelyan. It seemed a little rash to be talking to me of such things, for she hardly knew me and I was certain that the Captain would not have wished to be the subject of gossip.

6

The next morning, I wondered whether to tell Captain Trevelyan about my conversation with Madame Veronique. At worse she was giving away state secrets and at best she was indiscreet, just as mother might describe her for such candour. Either way, she should not have told me that the Captain was working behind enemy lines before he was shot around the time of the D-Day landings. So, when I saw him for my next lesson I decided not to repeat what Veronique had said, but instead I told him about a TV series I had seen a couple of years ago. Ron Randell starred in O.S.S., a programme shown on ITV each week, I explained.

The Office of Strategic Services operated behind Nazi lines in occupied France and the hero, Captain Frank Hawthorne, parachuted down as the opening credits rolled on each episode. A hushed voice told viewers that this is an agent of the OSS, en-route to a mission behind enemy lines. One of the nameless, faceless army, who fought the lonely war – the silent war. To this day, stories untold of heroes unknown. This is a mission from the annals of the Office of Strategic Services – the OSS.

"Very interesting," he said in a very uninterested voice. "But how are the stories untold if they are now appearing on

TV and how are the heroes unknown, if they are now being portrayed by Rob Randall?"

"Ron Randell," I corrected him. "He probably pronounced it Ran-dell, because there was another actor called Tony Randall, who was more famous than he was."

As we spoke, I walked around the room gazing at the incredible number of books that lined the walls. As I did so, I could not help noticing that the wire aerial connected to his radio stretched upwards and was pinned along one side of the window frame.

"Right," answered the Captain, without gaining any enthusiasm for the conversation. "But I haven't watched TV since someone invited me to a viewing of the Queen's Coronation in 1953. I wasn't impressed, so haven't bothered since."

But do you think there were nameless agents fighting a lonely war behind Nazi lines?"

"Oh," he stammered, as he slid a book from the shelf on the far side of the room. "I am certain there were, Peter. But I don't think they parachuted in on a weekly basis."

Discretion is the better part of valour, my mother always said, so I decided not to probe my witness any further on the subject.

"Why do you pin your aerial up the wall by the window?" I asked.

"It improves the reception."

The English lesson focused on nouns, verbs, adverbs and adjectives and my homework was to describe five people I had met since arriving in Berck and underline all the adjectives in the piece.

On my way down to the basement for lunch, I stopped to look at the journal, wondering whether the Pearsons had taken any notice of my petition for entries in the book. I had placed it on the sideboard that stood in the hallway and left it open, on the next unused page.

Lovely town and wonderful beach.
Much better than my last visit here in June 1944
Trevor and Doreen Pearson – 23/7/64.

I went to the courtyard garden and sat in that silent and totally secluded place at the rear of the house, thinking on Veronique's words. The feast days of Saint Agnes and Saint Mark had passed in February and April, she told me, so it was too late for great revelations this year. If I was still here next February, I asked if she would be able to tell me who I would marry when I grew up. But she said the myrtle berries only worked for young women, not boys like me.

The homework I had been set did provide an opportunity to describe the Captain and include the information that Veronique had given me about him. If he challenged it, I would confess it was all hearsay evidence, but at least it might provoke him to admit that he was an OSS officer in the less-than-great war.

Gretel was enjoying herself in the courtyard and ran up and down the airy steps until she slumped on the kitchen floor exhausted, but still gnawing on an old tennis ball. When she recovered, the puppy scampered around the basement, sniffing each piece of furniture and recognising only the smell of mother's scent and my perspiration. It was as if she had to identify and memorise each tiny part of our living quarters, until they were fully registered in her head. Did she think in French, I wondered, and how long would it take her to learn English.

When Friday arrived, mother excused herself from her teaching duties, because she had sheets to wash and iron before the new guests arrived the following day. That morning, I decided to take Gretel on a different route and set off towards the Town Hall, where there was apparently a market on Tuesdays, although I doubted it would be anything like the markets back home in England.

Halfway along the road was a cinema, situated on a corner, called Le Cinos. It appeared to be a fairly new structure and I guessed the original building must have been destroyed in the war. I looked at the bill posters to see if I recognised any of the films being shown. As far as I could make out, there were two films being shown on different days of the week. One was called *L'homme di Rio* and the other was *Becket*, which appeared to be an English language film with Richard Burton in the lead role. But the poster was in French and I assumed the movie itself would have been dubbed into that language.

Mum and I often went to the cinema in England, but I never went with Dad. If I went out with my dad, it was always for a drive in his latest car or to Upton Park to watch West Ham play. Mum had taken me to see *Jason and the Argonauts* a few months ago and I had pestered her to take me to see *From Russia with Love*, which all the kids in school were talking about. But she refused, saying it was unsuitable for someone of my age. Instead we went to see

Death drums on the river, which I had hoped would be a western film, but it wasn't; it was some dreary English-made adventure movie. Dad didn't like the cinema. In fact, I think the whole concept of fiction and storytelling was lost on him. He had taken Mum to the cinema a couple of times when I was small, to see classic films like *El Cid* and *Ben Hur*, but he always used to say that he couldn't take Charlton Heston seriously any more. Whenever he saw him in a TV film, he moaned that he only ever saw El Cid or Ben Hur and couldn't see Charlton Heston or any of his new characters. I said it was because he was such a good actor, but Dad was convinced Charlton Heston was a terrible actor and he would always be El Cid, galloping along the beach, strapped dead to his horse.

"That bit didn't take much acting, did it?" he roared. "I could have done that!"

I must have been remembering that scene because, without thinking, I turned right and headed back in the direction of the beach. It was only a short distance and soon Gretel was chasing a ball and tugging me along behind her. She looked tired out after fifteen minutes, so I decided to call in on Veronique Fournier on the way home, to show her how the puppy was getting on. It would also give Gretel a chance to cool down, or I could see myself getting a telling off from Mum.

I asked Veronique how she knew that Captain Trevelyan had been operating behind enemy lines in the war. She told me that he had been shot after parachuting onto the beach a few nights before the D-Day landings. Whilst Berck was some way north of the beaches used for the assault, the

Captain was a member of an elite squad who were used to send information from behind enemy lines. Veronique had nursed Trevelyan at the Maritime Hospital when he finally broke his cover after the landings in Normandy had proved successful. She was just as forthcoming about Ludwig von Tench.

"How long has he been here in Berck?" I asked.

"Since the war, the second world war, not the first one, like me."

"So he was here all through the war and stayed on?"

She thought for a moment.

"No, France had been occupied for about three years when he arrived in Berck. He was Leutnant von Tench in those days, but he was promoted soon after his arrival. He became Hauptmann von Tench, which means head man in German, it is the rank of Captain, he was a member of the general staff, not really the head man in the way you might think of it in England."

"Is it not strange that he stayed here after the war ended?" I asked. "After all, he was a German."

"If I tell you," she whispered, "you must promise not to tell Ludgwig I told you."

I nodded and wondered whether she wanted me to swear the oath. She didn't; the nod of my head was sufficient for her to continue telling me that von Tench had become disenchanted with the Nazi regime.

"He became sympathetic to our cause."

"Your cause?" I asked.

"He began feeding information to the French Resistance. He was, effectively, a British Agent. Some say he was the point of contact for Captain Trevelyan when he parachuted into our small town in 1944, because they have become good friends since."

I told Veronique about the television series OSS and she said it sounded very much like the real thing. But she was not aware of any American soldiers parachuting in to Berck, although there were very many, she said, amongst those who landed on the Normandy beaches. I needed to go home for my dinner and so excused myself and promised to come back again soon.

"How are your first guests?" she asked as I was leaving.

"They go home to England today," I answered. "Then we have a French family arriving on Saturday for a week. And, the week after that, a man is staying with us on his own, I think." I hesitated, trying to remember his name. "I think he is called Ben Avram, and Ben is an English name, so he doesn't sound very French to me."

"Because he is not," she replied, and I knew from the tone of her voice that she recognised the name. "Nor is he English." She sighed heavily. "Kaleb Ben Avram is Jewish, a regular visitor to our small town, one of a number of devout Nazi hunters, who roam this world with a single-minded aim, to root out Nazi war criminals and bring them to justice. I shall tell you more of him when you next visit me." She paused, wondering whether to add something. "It is important that you know about this man."

When I arrived at the beach, I needed to keep Gretel on the lead because there was still a danger that she would run away, which meant the only way she could chase a ball was if I chased it with her. The beach wasn't crowded like those

I had visited in England. The sand ran out towards the horizon and stretched for what looked like a mile in each direction.

As we came up the steps to the promenade to go home, there sitting on a bench with a thermos flask and some sandwiches, sat the Captain and von Tench. I said hello in French and they smiled and replied in English.

"Does the tide never come in?" I asked.

They both went to speak at once, but Trevelyan won the duel and explained how the tide had receded further from the shoreline over a long period of time. It made the beach perfect for flying a kite, he said, before asking if I had one.

"It isn't something I have ever had much enthusiasm for," I answered.

"It is one of those occupations," replied the German, "that seems to have no real purpose."

"It requires a great deal of skill," the Captain suggested with enough authority to indicate he had flown a kite at some time in his childhood.

"A bit like parachuting," I added, thinking back to what Madame Fournier had told me. I looked at the Captain to see if my comment changed his expression in any way. It did not. "Like one of the OSS agents I told you about," I added. "Who worked behind enemy lines. One of the nameless, faceless army, who fought the lonely war."

Von Tench looked at me with a furrowed brow. Not party to my previous conversation with the Captain, and not told about it either it seems.

"I took Gretel to see Madame Fournier on the way here."

"You should treat what Veronique says with a pinch of salt," replied Trevelyan.

"She has a vivid imagination," added von Tench.

When I returned home, I sat in the shadiest part of the courtyard to do my English homework and Gretel did likewise. She jumped up to follow me into the house when I suddenly remembered the visitor journal. The Pearsons had left, but not before they had written a second entry in the book.

We enjoyed our stay.
The beaches are just as I remember them.
Weather was very good. Sunny and no rain.
We hope to return again one day.
Trevor and Doreen – 24/7/64.

I was rather hoping for something a little more adventurous than such a bland record. I assumed that Trevor Pearson had fought in France during the war and was, perhaps, part of the D-Day landings. Why could he not write something about that? Why does someone with such an exciting past wish to talk about the beaches and the weather? I wondered whether I was thinking more about Captain Trevelyan than Trevor Pearson. Why should I not believe what Madame Fournier told me? Were her poor remembrances really an elaboration of past events, or was it simply that the Captain did not want me to know about what had, or should have been long forgotten.

I began to write the descriptions of five people I had met since arriving in Berck. I chose to describe Bruno as tall, with a good head of fair hair that was cut short around his ears. He wore a blue and white striped apron and smiled a lot. He spoke fluent English and French and seemed a very genuine character, someone you might trust instinctively. I underlined *tall, good, fair short, blue, white, striped, fluent* and *genuine*. I then moved on to his mother and described Veronique as likeable, approachable and someone who treated me like an adult, rather than a child. She was very old and had been a nurse in the war. I explained about her rather closeted lifestyle and underlined the adjectives I had used.

When it came to writing about Ludwig von Tench, I deliberately omitted the information that Veronique had given me about him. And I found I was at risk of using the same adjectives I had used for others. Finding a greater variety of adjectives was obviously the challenge that Captain Trevelyan envisaged when he set me this homework. It was a trick, in a way, because now I could not describe von Tench as approachable as I had done with Veronique. I had to find some other way to capture that part of his character. I plumped for well disposed, adding a description based on the picture in the lobby of Terry Williams flats.

I felt some empathy for the German, which was strange really, as I had spent most of my childhood shooting German soldiers on the bombed debris that littered the East End of London. I had never actually met one, but was completely prepared to kill them in our enactments of wartime battles. Ludwig may have looked like a German and still had that inflection in his voice that identified him as one too, but I liked him. He was very likeable, I was about to write, until I realised that I had used this same word for Veronique.

Captain Trevelyan must have known that I had only really got to know four people since we arrived. Bruno, his mother, and our two tenants would obviously be four of the five people I would write about. So, had he deliberately instructed me to write about five people, knowing I would struggle to find a fifth person? Or, was it done to ensure that I had to write about him? Was it some clever ploy to find out what Veronique had said about him? If it was, then it worked very well. The Captain was easy to describe; his smart appearance and Ronald Colman moustache, his fob watch and limp came easily to mind. And yet, his actual characteristics, his personality, were hidden beneath the surface, waiting to be uncovered. He was resolute, a deep thinker of subjects ignored by others, and I mentioned these attributes. But I also mentioned the things that Veronique had told me. The Captain was a member of an elite squad of officers who were used to send information from behind enemy lines. He had been shot after parachuting onto the beach, a few nights before the D-Day landings, and had been treated for his wounds at the Maritime Hospital in Berck. As I wrote the words and underlined the adjectives, I wondered what reaction I might get from the rather austere man.

I had one more person to describe and decided to push on and finish my homework. I considered cheating a little by opting to write about Gretel, but thought the Captain might make me do the whole thing again. So it was a decision between the estate agent and the butcher. I decided on Fabrice Dubois and described him as the only person I had got to know who did not speak English. As a consequence, I could say very little about him, other than to describe his physical features; plump, balding, with excessively large hands and fingers that looked like a bunch of pork sausages. I didn't know what Fabrice did in the war, so there was little more I could add. I underlined the adjectives and read through the five descriptions. I found a couple more adjectives, underlined them and closed the exercise book.

As I sat in the shade, I wondered if the rosary that Veronique showed me the other day had been given to her by one of the nuns who lived here; one of those sad women who sat in this very courtyard, dreaming of another life. It puzzled me why, having shown me the rosary, the old woman had not told me where she got it from, or the story behind it for, in all other respects, she was a woman who spoke freely on all matters, keeping nothing from me and even trusting me with some information that I should keep to myself.

7

I was just leaving the house with Gretel the following morning, when the Remilly family came around the corner, with the husband carrying a suitcase in each hand. I knew it must be them, because it was unlikely that anyone else would be walking down our untidy backstreet carrying luggage and looking as if they had just arrived on holiday. I offered to help with the bags but Monsieur Remilly assured me that he was able to manage. So I ran on ahead, with the little legs of Gretel trying to keep up, and called out to let my mother know that the new guests had arrived. She arrived in the hall, wiping her hands on her apron and getting flustered about how she might communicate with our first French guests.

"Bonjour Madame," I said to the woman. "Comment allez vous."

I looked at the woman and then at the young girl standing next to her mother. She was about my age and incredibly pretty.

It was a fatal error. My pronunciation was so good that Madame Remilly began speaking very quickly in her native tongue. Fortunately, her husband saw my distress and the look of bewilderment on my mother's face, and began talking in broken, but adequate English.

As I looked at the girl, I knew that everything I had previously thought about love had been utter nonsense. Those love trysts and party dates I had been on were simply an infant version of true love. True love was what I was feeling at this very moment, I told myself.

It occurred to me, in that instant, that I had known this fact all along. Maureen Stannard had not just loved me, not me alone, but another boy before me and probably another one since; and she had been in and out of love with Cliff Richard, in and out of love with Elvis, and Bobby Vee, and Dion and was now irrevocably in love with Paul McCartney. Well, that couldn't be love could it? Love must have a more enduring quality than a winter's day snowman, that melts in less time than it takes to build him. Love is a one-way door, with no exit sign in sight, it is not one of these new revolving doors you find up in London. One minute I was Maureen's *amore* and the next I was as annoying as the scratching sound of chalk on a blackboard.

Now it all made complete sense. None of that was love. This was love, what I was feeling now. Love, I confessed to myself, was what I felt about.....

I realised I didn't know her name.

"Je m'appelle Pierre. Enchante d'avoir fait votre connaissance."

Of course, I directed the words at the family, not just the incredibly pretty girl. Thank you, oh thank you Ludwig von Tench, I thought.

My French pronunciation was so poor that the entire Remilly family, in unison, reverted to the smattering of English they had learned. And, through this stroke of luck, I discovered the name of my first true love. Louane, Louane Remilly; it even sounded like someone you would fall in love with. Maureen Stannard sounded like a name from the school register, which meant no more to me now than Terry Williams.

"Le chien est Gretel."

Louane laughed. I had made Louane laugh. The joy welled up in my chest.

"La chienne nom est Gretel," Louane corrected me.

I would only find out later why she had laughed. Had I really given my boy dog a girl's name?

My mum showed them the room and I explained to Louane, in a version of English that was based on painting by numbers, about the visitor journal in the hallway.

"Write," I said, elongating the word beyond its single syllable, whilst performing a mime of writing on a non-existent book. "Write anything you like." My rather small vocabulary of mimes evaporated. How do you mime 'write whatever you like'?

As I lay in bed that night, I produced a list of interesting questions to ask Louane when I got another chance to speak to her. I would also need to get von Tench to teach me a few French phrases that might come in useful.

I awoke the next morning and sneaked quietly along the hallway from my bedroom, to take a peek at the visitors' journal, to see if Louane had written anything.

Arrived in Berck – very sunny.
Met a wonderfully interesting young man
can't wait for him to snog me!

71

Unfortunately, the entry I had imagined as I lay in bed last night remained just that – a figment of my testosterone driven imagination. The last entry in the book was still that of Mr Pearson, recording the weather and hoping he would return one day. I left the book open and made sure the pen still had ink in it. Then I listened at the door to see if the new guests had got up yet.

"Are the Remillys not up yet?" I asked Mum as she placed a plate of toast on the table.

"They were up very early. They had a picnic basket and everything. It looked to me, as if they may have set off towards the beach."

I checked to make sure that our promised visit to the beach was still on and went up to change my shirt. Mum was waiting in the hall for me when I came down. She looked at me a little strangely, wondering, I suppose, why I had changed my shirt. Thankfully, she didn't ask; or perhaps she already knew.

It occurred to me on the way to the beach that any message Louane did choose to write in the visitors' journal was likely to be in French. I grabbed some paper and a pen and started compiling a list of words I would need to raise at my next French lesson with von Tench. Just then, as I was thinking about the quirky old man, there he was, walking towards us with a small shopping bag in one hand and a newspaper in the other. Out of politeness, mother stopped to talk to him and asked where he originally came from.

"Munich," he replied, "but I have not been there since the war."

Mother mentioned our new guests and he put his bag of shopping on the ground, which suggested we might be here for some time. So I decided to join the conversation and interrupted them, much to their surprise, suggesting that my French lessons had now taken on greater urgency, if we were to make our new guests welcome at the Convent.

"Perhaps I could learn some appropriate questions or sayings, like 'do you like the beach?' 'Or would you like me to show you around?'"

Of course, I had calculated that, from this combination of sentences, I should be able to ask Louane if she would like me to take her to the beach.

"I might also need some assistance from you Mr von Tench, to interpret the visitors' journal should she, er, should they write something in it."

Just as they were preparing to cross examine me, Captain Trevelyan came along the road behind us.

"Good morning," he said to us and then looked at von Tench. "I just wanted to remind you to get some eggs."

It was in that moment that the relationship of the two old men gained perfect clarity for me. Why was von Tench buying eggs for both of them? Perhaps they just shared them, after all, it would take each of them twice as long to eat six eggs than three eggs each. My mind whirred. I was trying to find some other excuse for the Captain's last statement. It could be perfectly innocent, although this option was slipping back down the list of possible explanations. I looked at my mother's face for any indication of shock. But there was none. Had she missed the significance of the Captain's remark or was she even more tolerant than I gave her credit for? Were the two men living together? I know the boys in my class got quite a lot of things wrong when it came to sex, but was it not illegal to be a homo or queer as they called them?   Would she really place the important issue of my education in the hands of two lawbreaking homosexuals?

When we eventually reached the beach, Mum sat on the promenade and I took Gretel for a walk. I had deliberately coaxed my eager bloodhound to smell the scent of Louane from outside the guest bedroom in the hall and now she would search out and find the new love in my life. After twenty minutes, Gretel had managed to track down and locate six other dogs, an empty Coke bottle and a towel that seemed to belong to nobody. Perhaps it was Louane's towel I thought and she had gone swimming. The only thing was, the sea was still probably a mile from where we were standing and, at that rate, it wouldn't be deep enough to swim in until you got to Cornwall.

The rules seemed to change in France. Every Sunday at home, we would tuck into roast beef, with roast potatoes, vegetables, Yorkshire pudding and gravy. In England, this never changed. It was as if it was the law in England, and everyone had to comply.

When I went out to play in London on Sundays, all I could smell was the odour of the Sunday roast wafting from every house I passed. Every oven in London was set at gas mark 4.   That smell was unforgettable, along with the accompaniment of the *beep, beep, beeeeeep* signal on the radio, and the ineluctable sound of *With a song in my heart,* blaring out of every open window along Grundy Street, quickly followed by the dulcet tones of Jean Metcalfe telling me it was time for lunch: *'The time in Britain is twelve noon, in Germany it's one o'clock, but home and away, it's time for Two-Way Family Favourites."*

And yet, in an instant, this was all brought to an end. The ramifications of our move to France were about to become tangible, edible even. Firstly, Mum wanted to recast the mould for Sundays, to transform the essence of Sunday, to silence the beep, beep, beeeep, the time in Britain is twelve noon, in France it's one o'clock, but now we're away, it's no longer roast beef, done just the way I liked it, with the gravy poured over the beef and potatoes, but never over the Yorkshire pudding, as that would make it soggy.

The mothers of the other kids I played with, could never remember how each of their kids liked things. But, being the only one meant you got everything just as you wished it to be; how could she forget where I liked my gravy poured because she couldn't get me confused with anyone else, I didn't have any brothers or sisters. Indeed, the ultimate advantage of not having a brother or a sister was having a decidedly non-soggy Yorkshire pudding. That Yorkshire pudding was a monolith of my mother's love for me. There are moments in our life that seem as permanent, as natural as breathing; they provide reassurance in a changing world. But, like most things that you try to hold on to for a long time, they slip from your grasp. Sooner, or later, you have to let go.

"I thought we could have some fish and chips for lunch today," said Mum, as if she was passing a comment about the weather.

It was in that moment that the enormity of our move to France seized my mind. Even the compensatory thought of seeing the lovely Louane evaporated in the smoky steam of a disappearing gravy boat.

"But it's Sunday," I replied and the thought was so overpowering that I didn't feel the need to add to that statement. I was ready to do something that Perry Mason would never consider – a plea bargaining arrangement. Why would he? His clients were never guilty anyway. But I was ready; I was prepared to accept a plea agreement on not listening to Jean Metcalfe, I would readily give up hearing Tommy Steele singing *Little White Bull* and Max Bygraves wittering on about a pink toothbrush. I would even forego the beep, beep, beeeep. But how would I survive without roast beef? How would I survive my mum remembering not to pour gravy on my Yorkshire pudding? How else would she demonstrate her undying motherly love for me?

Perry, help me out here; how can I turn this case around? But I couldn't. The case of the missing roast dinner was not going to end happily.

I tried to ignore that it was Sunday, but the church bells were ringing out. And yet the unthinkable happened. It was as unlikely as Perry Mason losing a case, but finally, I was forced to surrender. Fish and chips it would be, provided she didn't pour the tomato ketchup on the fish. However, things were about to go from bad to worse. In spite of the fact that we were close enough to the sea to catch the fish ourselves, fish was not the most popular thing to come out of the sea in Berck. That honour went to something called moule. Apparently for fish fried in batter, we would need to go to Étaples where the fishing fleets operated from.

We were tumbling downhill at high speed, escalating downwards from roast beef and Yorkshire pudding, to fish and chips, to something called moule and frites. How can I eat something I cannot spell, pronounce or even interpret? Where was von Tench when I needed him? How on earth do I order fish and chips in this country?

"Oh, come on Peter. Nothing ventured, nothing gained," said Mum, sounding a bit like Dad when West Ham were two-nil down at half time.

Or, put another way, I thought, something ventured, something gained, like gastroenteritis. All changes come with sadness, because we are saying goodbye to something and a part of us is lost in that goodbye. A piece of us must die before another piece of us can live on.

Mum had the moules and frites and I began plea bargaining arrangements with the waitress. Luckily she took a liking to my boyish charm and enchanting English accent, so was prepared to listen to my wish list for lunch.

"Hachis Parmentier," she declared, before adding "You – will – like – it."

"Shepherds pie," I told her when she placed the dish before me.

"What is shepherd?"

"Vieux homme," I replied, after giving the translation some thought.

Old man pie, she thought.

"Old – man? Non – it – is – beef."

She looked at me as if I was mad and returned to the kitchen.

Actually, the food was very tasty and perhaps even better than my mum's roast beef dinner, but I am not prepared to make a statement to that effect at this time, your honour. A new priority had taken prominence for my next French lesson. Yes, of course, I was still in love with the lovely Louane, but I will die if I don't master the language of food very quickly and secure a meal that resembles, even slightly, roast beef.

8

The next French lesson was not until Tuesday so I would need to wait one more day to resolve this most urgent of requirements. I could survive on Hachis Parmentier for another day, Monday morning was English with the Captain and I had other issues to resolve with him.

"If you were Ron Randell," I asked him, "would you parachute onto the incredibly vast beach in Berck, or would you parachute into the forest to the north of the aerodrome."

My attempt at learning about his past was dismissed in four words.

"How would I know?"

I tried to fathom the tone of that answer. Did he suspect that I knew he had parachuted behind enemy lines as Veronique had told me? Or was he confirming his earlier statement that I should not believe anything the woman says?

I abandoned my first line of enquiry and moved on to the matter of his sexuality. How would Perry raise such a delicate matter.

"How do you know when you are in love; how do you know when you have met the right person?" I deliberately substituted 'person' for 'girl' and I wondered if he had noticed the subtlety of my phraseology.

"Why do you ask?"

"Well, I've never been in love before and I think I might be, but it's given me an upset stomach. I simply wanted to make sure whether it is love, or just a dodgy Hachis Parmentier."

He laughed.

"If you had the Parmentier in Le Voltaire, then you are probably in love, because they have a very good chef there. Love sometimes hurts, it can make you ill, but it is always good."

"Have *you* ever been in love?"

"I have a book here that might help," he replied, without answering the question. "It's a children's book; some might consider the subject too young for you, but it is particularly well written, especially the chapter where the velveteen rabbit asks an elderly toy what 'real' is. Read it and it will help you understand what love is. Now, let us look at your English homework."

He opened the exercise book and began silently reading the descriptions of the five people I had chosen to write about. I felt a little bit nervous, trying to work out when he would arrive at the section on himself. He maintained an expressionless face throughout and simply circled two or three adjectives that I had failed to identify. There was no comment on the assertions I had made about his wartime career. To him, this was just writing; simply a group of words to enable me to understand the difference between verbs and adjectives.

So, after two hours of more adjectives, verbs, nouns, pronouns and adverbs, I was ready for lunch. Homework, the Captain told me was another essay, this time on Berck sur mer. It seems that the scope of my essays is projected outwards, firstly with the house, then the town; so I guess France was next.

"Does it need to be true or false?"

"Fact or fiction," he corrected me. "You choose; whichever you prefer to write."

When I returned downstairs to read the book he had given me, I had high hopes that it would resolve the question about my teacher's sexuality. But it didn't throw any light on his feelings, only my own. You become real, the toy rabbit was told, when someone loves you, not just for a few days, not just over Christmas, but for a long time. So, perhaps I wasn't in love with Louane after all; perhaps I hadn't yet become real.

"Are there different laws in France?" I asked Mum over lunch.

"I don't think so. Why do you ask?"

"No reason, I just wondered."

After lunch, I crept into the hallway to look in the visitors' journal, before going to the courtyard to do my homework.

c'est formidable d'être à nouveau ici
aller à la plage à pied;

The handwriting looked very much like that of a child. I wondered what it might mean. This new boy in my life is formidable; that was possible. Then von Tench came in the door, carrying a small bag of shopping.

"I am trying to interpret the entry in the journal," I said, sounding as if I was wandering around the country looking for words to translate.

"What do you think it means?" he asked, looking at the writing.

"Something is new and formidable."

"And what is formidable," he asked.

"Daunting, a brave person; a chivalrous knight can be formidable or daunting."

"Dauntless, more likely."

He began to walk off but I asked him what it said.

"They are happy to be back in Berck again and had a nice walk to the beach."

"So, she hasn't met anyone particularly nice then?"

He looked at me for a moment and went upstairs. Whatever thoughts were going through my mind, they were definitely fiction.

I sat in the courtyard garden reading *The Velveteen Rabbit*, which did not take long as it was a story for smaller children in quite large print. It was a hot day and I felt good sitting in the shade, so I decided to make a start on the essay. I had an idea that might prise a little more information out of the Captain and began to write an essay based on an episode of the television programme OSS called Operation Foul Ball. Captain Frank Hawthorne had parachuted into some unknown location in France. He was operating undercover as a deserter hoping to join a French resistance group and blow up a bridge.

Even though I was sure that Captain Trevelyan had not seen any episodes of OSS, let alone this particular one, I decided to change a couple of the elements in the story. There was no reason why the unknown location in France could not be Berck sur mer, and the resistance group could easily have been trying to blow up the airfield outside town. Captain Frank Hawthorne was given another name, as was the Operations of Strategic Service, but the French resistance, I decided, needed to remain the same, otherwise the story would make no sense at all.

In the end, simply blowing up an airfield did not fill the first page, so there were elements of rescue added to the sabotage mission which also included blowing up an experimental laboratory and the distribution of newsletters about Nazi atrocities by the Gestapo. For the sake of realism and because I suspected Captain Trevelyan might raise the question, the undercover agent escaped back to Britain on a fishing boat from Étaples.

I hooked the lead on to the collar on Gretel's neck and took her into the hallway, allowing her to sniff the Visitors' Journal for any hints of Louane. Then we set off for a long beach walk. The breeder had told us that, the wirehaired fox terrier had a strong hunting instinct and I tried reminding Gretel of this as we searched for our prey. We never found the Remilly family that day and it was a long trudge back from the far end of the beach.

"She's only a puppy, Peter," said my mum when we finally arrived home. "You mustn't tire her out too much."

Ludwig von Tench sounded quite angry when I traipsed up the stairs for my lesson the following morning. Something had upset him because when I asked if we could have a French lesson again, he insisted it was time for some history. Perhaps questioning his decision was a bad idea on my part, but he did not hide his feelings when I suggested I could benefit from learning some conversational French.

"I am the teacher and you are the student. And I object to teaching the French language by order; food, then shopping and now how to chat up a girl. There is a method to learning a language and it is not dictated by circumstance."

As it turned out, I had very little use for conversational French because I hardly saw the evasive Louane. I took every opportunity to walk Gretel along the promenade and around the streets of Berck, but never saw where the Remilly family spent the larger part of their holiday.

9

By the time Friday arrived, I had given up any hope of ever having a conversation with our young visitor, the lovely Louane, and after an even longer walk with Gretel and yet another missed arithmetic lesson, I sat reading in the courtyard garden. This tiny oasis, separated from the bustling world outside, was a beautiful place, trapped in time, and evocative of a different age.

Do buildings have memories? Someone once told me that oak trees never forget anything and yet buildings see so much more of life than a tree might do. Imagine what St. Paul's Cathedral has seen, or the Tower of London, all that pageant, all those executions. And, what has this tiny courtyard seen? Monks and nuns of ancient times past, fasting, praying, dreaming of other worlds, celestial and otherwise. Buildings must have memories for, if memories are lost to us as time passes, where do they go?

My memories are imbedded in our cranky old house in Poplar, the one we lived in up to two years ago. We were just a ship's horn blast from the busy River Thames and we heard that poignant sound every New Year's Eve. Across the street was a bombsite, a debris, the remnants of buildings destroyed in the Blitz, the shattered bricks and rubble still clinging to memories of a distant Regency era.

And other more recent memories, are deposited in the ground floor maisonette that we moved into two years ago. The kids at school wanted to know which councillor my dad had bribed to get the new place, but I didn't know him well enough to ask. It was around the time he came back from Spain and it seemed strange how I had forgotten him in such a short time. I wanted to have missed him as much as Mum had. I wanted to throw my arms around him, just as she did. But you can't make yourself feel things that aren't natural. Love must come as easily as petals to a flower. Sadly, or strangely not so sadly, I felt the same way when he died. Not an emptiness but, paradoxically, something tangible that was absent from my emotions. I didn't feel that same sadness that Mum felt, because she cried a lot and, for some ridiculous reason, I couldn't manage a single tear. I think it might have been due to the suddenness. I did not see him fall ill, I didn't see him die, I didn't go to the funeral. I didn't see any evidence that he had died, so perhaps that is why I failed to shed any tears. Maybe my sub-conscious didn't accept that he was dead.

His passing was all so clinical, as if he was being filed away, the memory of him stored in the two houses we had lived in and in some Spanish apartment that I had never seen. Yes, the buildings would remember him, because I couldn't, or wouldn't because, with each day, he slipped further and further away.

Mum missed him though. That weekend we went to my grandparents' house, when granny tired of playing Ludo, I went upstairs to read, while the grown-ups discussed my father's death, I suppose. They didn't hear me come down the stairs to the kitchen. Nor did they know I listened to their conversation at the serving hatch.

"You must learn to live without him, Sue," granddad said, but Mum just cried. "We none of us know what the future holds. Perhaps you will find someone else, you're still a very young woman."

"No," she replied between the tears. "I couldn't do that to anyone because, one night, in that future which nobody can see into, I will be in the arms of that other man and I will call him Pete by mistake, and I wouldn't want to do that to anyone."

I shared the memory of that moment with the serving hatch. I hadn't known, before then, just how much my mum loved my dad. I loved him too, of course. If nothing else, he was unpredictable. One day he arrived home in a red sports car and wanted to take me for a drive. Mum was too busy to go with us and we drove all the way to Epping Forest, where we once went to on a Green Line bus. I was really looking forward to exploring the woods, but I ended up sitting outside the Wakes Arms pub for two hours, eating cheese and onion crisps and drinking bottles of Pepsi, while Dad sat inside with a friend of his who just happened to turn up in the same pub.

After my grandparents had left, I asked Mum what Dad died of and she just said it was a sudden illness. I decided not to press the matter because it obviously upset her and I didn't want to hurt her by asking too many questions. My endless questioning was the cause of some distress to Mum, and granny had specifically asked me not to ask too many questions because it would only upset my mum.

"We have to think about little Peter now, Sue," I heard granny tell Mum from the other side of that serving hatch, and I crept back upstairs. This was more or less the same advice granny gave me before she kissed me goodbye. "We have to think of your mum now, Peter."

As I sat in the courtyard garden, that weekend with my grandparents seemed a long time ago, but barely a few weeks had passed. I wanted to pause life's endless voyage for a moment and consider why we had moved house to France. And yet, it was such an enormous question, with no obvious answer, that I knew it would occupy too much of my time to solve the mystery. I could ponder on the subject for eternity and yet I might never discover the true answer. I might discover *an* answer, but it might just be another version of the truth, and not the actual truth at all. So I put the thought out of my mind, planting it somewhere in the intricate brickwork of the courtyard garden, in order that its myrtle-covered walls might consider it over many, many centuries, until it resolved the case of the unexpected relocation. It wasn't difficult to think of an alternative subject to pursue.

I embarked on a new topic of meditation and began wondering, whilst sitting in the courtyard, whether Louane had stayed in this house before, or did the entry in the journal simply imply that they had been to Berck before? I decided that it made no difference anyway. She was going home tomorrow, wherever home was for the Remilly family. The lessons on Tuesday and Thursday addressed European history, rather than the French language, and the only progress I had made in this direction was the ability to order roast beef – a complete waste of time, because it was not a dish the French were familiar with and it certainly wasn't accompanied by Two-way Family Favourites.

"Are we getting a telephone?" I asked Mum, as she was getting herself ready to go out.

"Probably. I need to find out how we go about it."

There seemed little chance of us being allocated a telephone number in time for me to pass it on to Louane before she left. And she might consider me a little stupid if I asked for her number when I didn't even have a telephone of my own.

"What about a radio?" I asked, chancing my arm.

She shook her head. I only had a few weeks to get my mum to buy a radio because the football season would be starting soon and hopes were high after my team, West Ham had won the FA Cup only a couple of months ago. I watched the game on TV. Dad only took me to one match last season, when we beat Leyton Orient in the League Cup at Upton Park. Now, the club would be in the European Cup Winners Cup next season and I was living in Europe.

"If West Ham play in France, can I go to watch the match, Mum?"

"France is a big country Peter, it's not like hopping on a bus to Upton Park."

My mother had excused herself from teaching duties again before heading off to the shops. And I had retired to the courtyard armed with an exercise book containing the multiplication tables on the back cover. I put it next to me on the bench and decided to read the last two chapters of *Kim* instead. Then, without any sound or warning, Gretel suddenly leapt to her feet and barked. Louane was standing on the step holding a book of her own.

I looked at Gretel sternly, then quickly changed that look and smiled at Louane.

"Oh, I am sorry," she said in perfectly acceptable English. "I thought you had lesson with one of the upstair gentleman."

Okay, there was a distinct misunderstanding of plural words and the last two words should have been the other way round, but she spoke English! And she spoke it to me.

"The gentlemen upstairs." I replied, trying not to sound condescending. "No, not on Friday. On Friday I learn maths, arithmetic, but my mother has something else to do. So I am reading." I enunciated each word, deliberately pronouncing every syllable separately, individually.

I held up the book and she coyly looked down at the one she held in her hand. She mumbled something and turned to go.

"You can read here if you like," I told her.

"I don't want to," she answered.

My heart slumped. But, she was only trying to think of a word.

".... disturb you," she continued. "I don't want to disturb you."

"No, that is okay. We can read here together, or we could go for a walk." My index and middle finger were made to walk along the arm of the seat.

Gretel jumped up at the sound of the word *walk*.

"She speaks English," I said to Louane, but pointing at Gretel. "Well, understands it I mean, she can't actually speak English, or French."

"Marche," the girl said to the puppy who had now sprung into life.

"As in *march*," I replied. "That's very convenient. Some of the French language is the same, and some of it is very different."

"Like dog or friend – chien, ami."

"Mon chien," I replied. "Mon ami."

I dived in with both feet and asked if she wanted to take the dog for a walk. It was a trick I had learned from Perry Mason.

"Yes," she said.

"With me?" I added.

It turned out that Louane was very easy to talk to. As we walked along the Rue Carnot towards the beach, I told her about my father dying, our journey to France and what Veronique had told me about Captain Trevelyan. But I didn't mention the fact that I thought he might be homosexual, in case she wondered how I might have known that about someone. Louane lived on the outskirts of Paris and they had visited Berck a couple of times before. Her parents had also taken her to Lake Annecy, and last year they went to a coastal town called Honfleur, but it didn't have a beach, just a harbour area, where passenger and freight boats travelled from Paris to the sea. She made her holidays sound far more interesting than my own reminiscences about Southend-on-Sea and Cromer.

"We haven't got a telephone yet," I told her, adding that we hoped to get one soon. I am not sure Louane understood the intention of such a statement, because she didn't offer to give me her telephone number. There seemed little point, I suppose, as we hardly knew each other.

The following morning the Remilly family left shortly after I finished breakfast. But I waited around in order that I could say goodbye. I didn't ask her for their address; she knew mine, of course, in case she wanted to write to me.

On reflection, it might not have been love after all. I did miss her that evening and the feeling was certainly different to any other I had felt, but it wasn't love, not real love, for it didn't hurt enough when she left.

Loveley vacation – hope to see you next year

Lovely was spelled incorrectly and the use of the word vacation suggested she was learning English from an American source, but she hoped to see me next year. All I had to do now was survive another year without roast beef and Yorkshire pudding.

10

It had been a week since I last visited Veronique. Walking the dog had taken on a different objective during Louane's stay at the convent guest house. Even Gretel had begun to wonder why our walks had extended beyond the house in Rue de la Plage and along a one-mile stretch of sand, before returning home the long way, via the Rue Carnot, in case our guests had stopped for a drink in one of the coffee shops along that road. But yesterday afternoon, I did stop at Veronique's house, just to say hello and let her see how Gretel was progressing. She didn't seem very well, so I decided not to stay too long.

Berck was busier at weekends. People who lived in the surrounding towns and villages would arrive by train or car, in large numbers, to sit on the beach, fly kites, build sandcastles and eat moule en frites. I was getting used to frites instead of chips, but mussels were never going to replace fried fish, or even fish fingers. Mum tried her best to produce a traditional Sunday roast, but it proved difficult with the ingredients available to her.

"Will granny and granddad be coming over to see us sometime?"

"Yes, in a couple of weeks."

"Can they bring us a supply of gravy powder and custard powder and perhaps a few other items to remind us of home?"

She nodded and offered to buy me an ice cream on the front to cheer me up.

"Our new guest arrives tomorrow. Try not to bother him too much, Peter, as I think he is on business rather than on holiday. He may not have time to chat, and he may not want to write things in the Visitors' Journal."

Mum knew I would agree to almost anything whilst eating a cornet.

"How was Madame Fournier when you visited her yesterday afternoon?"

"Actually, she wasn't very well. She had pains in her stomach."

"Well, we had better check with Bruno on the way home, just to make sure he is aware of it. She may need to see a doctor."

As we walked back down the Rue Carnot, I tried to remember whether there had been anything significant about my visit to Veronique yesterday afternoon, just in case Bruno asked me any questions.

I remembered that Gretel had been quite relieved to get a rest halfway through our walk, and Veronique was very pleased to see us. There was no TV in her house, but the radio was always on, normally playing quite loudly, although she turned it down a little so that she could hear me speak, because I don't think she had very good hearing. The room suddenly went quiet when the radio was turned down and I could hear her stomach rumbling loudly.

"What is happening in England," I asked, wondering if it was the BBC news she had been listening to.

"The Vietnam war and race riots in the United States."

I wanted to tell her that neither Vietnam, nor the United States were in England, but I was sure she knew this already.

"Do you get the football results?"

"Saturday evenings, but I didn't hear them this week."

"No, the football season has ended. I was just wondering how I would find out the results when the season begins again. What about the cricket?"

"Yes," she answered encouragingly. "That was on the radio earlier. I don't like cricket, but it reminds me so much of home that I leave it on, in the background. It struck me as strange that she still regarded England as her home.

England are playing Australia she told me and Australia got three hundred or more runs. This sounded like reasonable news until she remembered that it wasn't Australia who had scored three hundred runs, but one of their players.

"Someone named Simpson got over three hundred runs on his own."

That wasn't such good news, but at least I had a source of information from home and the sense of isolation eased a little.

Veronique got up out of her chair and was holding her stomach.

"Are you okay?" I asked.

"Just a pain in my stomach. I've had it for a while now."

She walked across the room and turned up the volume on the radio. The BBC news had just started and it was difficult to hear the man's voice through the crackling and scratching of the poor reception.

"You should run the aerial up along the window," I told her, sounding as if I knew what I was talking about. "It improves the reception."

She looked at me a little strangely, but just turned the tuning knob until the crackling eased a little. The newsreader could now be heard a little clearer:

'The two men appeared at the Central Criminal Court at the Old Bailey this morning, charged with the armed bank robbery that took place in Notting Hill High Street three weeks ago. A third man is wanted by the police in connection with the robbery. Police say that Richard Patterson, also known as Rickie Patterson is dangerous and should not be approached. Mister Patterson is described as forty-years-old, tall, auburn haired, with a beard. We now return you to Old Trafford for the second test match.'

"Do you want to listen to the Test Match?" she asked.

"Just to hear the latest score, then I should make my way home."

Veronique looked a little disappointed that I was leaving so soon. I guessed that she deliberately avoided asking me where I had been for the last week, because she didn't want me to look on my visits as an obligation. They were not that, of course, because she was an engaging woman whose candour and forthright speaking created conversations the like of which I had never known, largely because she saw no age barrier to our discussion.

She always began by saying that I reminded her of her son and, to be honest, I had taken very little notice of this until she called him her eldest son. I questioned it and she seemed surprised that I didn't know that she had an older son who had died during the war. His name was Laurent and he would have taken over the family business if he had survived the war. I suppose I may have reminded her of him because when you die, your features are suspended in time; people who die don't grow old, they don't wither and age, but remain eternally youthful. So, perhaps it was easier for her to remember him as a child – well, easier than it was to remember Bruno in that way.

Australia had six hundred runs in their first innings, so I suggested that she might want to turn the radio off now. She groaned again as she sat back down in the armchair.

"Are you still in pain?"

"A little," she replied and her stomach grumbled again.

"Shall I fetch your son?"

"No, no," she insisted. "He will only want me to go to the hospital."

"Well, perhaps you should, if you are unwell."

"It's nothing. Anyway, I have experience of hospitals and they are not the best places to be when you are feeling ill."

"But you were a nurse."

"Better to be in your own home. A little rest will put me right, thank you Peter."

The Second World War had not been kind to Veronique. That sounds blindingly obvious, for the war was unkind to a great many people and kind to none. But, she had lost both her husband and their eldest son and I couldn't imagine how such a loss must feel. She told me that Laurent was killed delivering bread to the canteen at the local aerodrome, where the Germans were based. I don't know why, but I just assumed he had been killed by the Germans and said something to this effect.

"No," she replied, "Laurent was killed in an allied bombing raid on the aerodrome."

It took a second for this to sink in; the British had killed her son. For a moment, I wondered if she felt any anger towards me, for his death, but she didn't, of course; I wasn't born then and she was English, just the same as I was. I could sense some pain in her voice, although this could have more tangible origins than the sadness she felt at her loss. But I changed the subject anyway, and told her about Louane. I needed to talk to someone about it and the old woman was as good a listener as a speaker. She seemed to understand how I might easily believe I was in love, when in fact I wasn't. The way she described the feeling, it was as if it happened every day, which made me feel normal, as it had never happened to me before.

I then told Madame Fournier how much I missed England and that I was finding it a little difficult to adapt to the food. I like roast beef, I explained and *proper* fish and chips. She thought for a moment and recalled a fish and chip shop where she came from in south London. A large cauldron of cooking fat sizzled away above a large coal fire, she told me, and long queues stretched along the road outside on a Friday evening, with chips wrapped up in an old newspaper, with steaming fish in crispy batter. She remembered it as if it was only yesterday.

"I love fish," she said, "but I know what you mean, it is different from the fish we got at home. No batter and they serve the fish whole, over here, head, tail and everything."

"And you eat it like that?"

"Oh, yes, mustn't waste any. With the little fish, you can eat the whole thing."

Her stomach grumbled and I wondered if she was remembering the fish and chips from back home in England or if the pain had returned.

Veronique enjoyed meeting Gretel and told me some interesting things about the war, although some of it sounded like gossip, rather than facts. My mum would have said she was indiscreet if I had repeated some of the things she told me, which I decided not to do so, in case she thought I was being led astray.

"Do they have the same laws in France as in England?" I asked the old woman.

She thought for a moment and confirmed that they did. Unlike mother, she asked why, and kept asking until I gave an answer. The other difference was that I could not mention the next thing to my mum as it was too embarrassing, but in the case of Veronique, she seemed to be different because nothing fazed her. There was no subject that was out of bounds with her, other than those I would prefer not to raise with a woman old enough to be my grandmother.

"In England, it is against the law to be a homosexual," I told her.

"Are you a homosexual?" Veronique asked me in a very matter-of-fact tone. I had learned that, in old age, a person becomes indifferent to almost everything; they become unshockable, blasé to whatever life threw at them.

"No!" I shouted a little too loudly. "Good grief no!" How loud did I need to shout to completely convince her that I wasn't queer?

"Then why do you ask?"

But, before she had finished her question, she had realised why my question had been asked. She didn't say she knew, but I could see the brightness return to her eyes. They seemed to smile at me. It was a look I recognised well from my mother's expressions. It was a second sense that women have, something other than anticipation, more like intuition.

"There are the same laws in France, but they have been decriminalised."

"So it is a crime but it is not criminal?" Did Perry Mason know about this I wondered?

"It is not a criminal act to be homosexual, not in France," she replied. "In France they believe that if there is no victim, then it cannot be a crime. They only punish true crimes, not artificial ones in France."

"So decriminalisation allows homosexuality?"

"Yes, but it prevents burning people at the stake for witchcraft as well. It does not punish superstition, but fact."

Perry Mason was always preaching about facts, so it sounded right. She could see I was mulling this over in my mind.

"And now," she said, "you want to know whether that is why Captain Trevelyan has remained in France all this time."

I could feel myself blushing, something I couldn't imagine in front of Veronique, because everything was so down-to-earth with her. Old age had liberated her from the risk of being outrageous. She was not, in the least bit judgemental, nor did she feel the need to guard against making an embarrassingly honest remark, like most adults do when talking to children.

"Well, it is not. He stayed here because he fell in love. In love with someone who was in France, and because he was in love with France and its people, just as I was. There is no difference."

Her final words 'there is no difference' echoed with relevance and truth. She meant that there was no difference between the love the Captain felt to the love she had felt for her husband, or indeed, how I felt for Louane, except Trevelyan's love had been made real.

"You don't think that the Captain is the traitor, do you?" I said, more as a statement than a question.

"I *know* he is not the traitor," she replied. "He was in a coma when the betrayal occurred, and I know that to be true too, because I put him in the coma."

"You put him in to a coma?"

"Yes, he was shot by the Germans when he landed at the edge of the woods and he was taken to the hospital where I worked as a nurse. The surgeons operated on him to remove the bullet but he was worried about being interrogated by the Gestapo, so I injected him with a barbiturate to induce a coma. I told the Germans that he had slipped into a coma during the operation and that he might wake up at any time. But I knew he would remain in that induced state of unconsciousness for some days."

Suddenly, she stopped talking and I could sense the fear that she was telling me too much. She told me that I should go home now, or my mother might start worrying about me.

Gretel sensed that our visit was coming to an end and jumped up, before Madame Fournier flinched in her chair. It was the second sense that dogs have, something other than anticipation, canine intuition. Veronique asked me to see myself out. I failed to notice that she did not want to get up because of the recurring pain in her stomach. I should have noticed that.

11

Bruno told us that his mother had suffered from the pains in her stomach for a few weeks but he could not get her to visit the doctor. In spite of being a nurse for most of her life, she had an aversion to hospitals, for she had witnessed so many people go in to one and never come out again.

The following morning, our new guest arrived whilst Mum and I were still eating breakfast. Mum got extremely flustered as she clearly wasn't expecting him to arrive so early. The room was ready of course, but Mum wasn't. I was despatched to find my exercise books before going up to see Captain Trevelyan and Mum showed Mr Avram his room before returning to the kitchen. She arrived back downstairs, still a little agitated, before I had left and Mum knew I was loitering with intent, as she put it.

"Captain Trevelyan will not be ready for me at this time," I told Mum.

"The Captain is always up early. Now get yourself upstairs for the lesson."

As I came back up to the hallway, the door to the guest room was open, so I crept towards it and tapped lightly on the open door. Mr Avram was a strange looking creature. I had seen others, like him, around certain parts of East London, particularly up near Whitechapel. I remember asking my grandmother about them, when we were on a bus heading up into London one day. She said they were orthodox Jews. I wanted to ask what an unorthodox Jew looked like because, presumably, they looked even more peculiar than the orthodox type.

Avram's smile was half-hearted and he scratched at his black beard as he waited for me to speak. In a quiet voice I explained to him about the journal. He must have wondered why I was whispering, but he didn't ask.

"I shall write something in it immediately," he answered loudly enough to be heard by my mother in the basement.

"Thank you," I said and rushed upstairs before mother appeared.

I wanted to tell him that he had missed the point. It was a visitors' journal and its purpose was to record information about their stay at the convent guest house. But I kept quiet, partly because I was a little unsure of the strange looking man, but also because I was interested to see what he would write so soon after arriving.

I lingered on the stairs long enough to see him complete the task and, in the absence of my mum arriving, I thanked him and headed up to the next floor where the Captain was waiting for me. I handed him my exercise book.

"My essay on Berck."

"Sit down," he replied and opened it.

"I finished *Kim*," I told him.

He pointed at a shelf on the far wall.

"See if you can remember where it came from."

I found the section of Rudyard Kipling books, but they didn't seem to be in alphabetical order."

"They're not..." I began to say.

"No," he interjected, completely understanding my unspoken statement. "They are in order of publication. Just leave it among the Kiplings and I will attend to it."

I thought about his answer for a moment. He wanted the books to be in the order that the author had written them. I looked at the books again, but that system didn't seem to fit the bill. Dickens, Hardy, Browning, the Bronte sisters, were all jumbled together, occupying nearly two full shelves of the longest wall. The Captain could see me staring at his filing system and could almost hear my mind whirring, like von Tench's scroll saw. I think he was hoping I would not work it out; if his system could be understood by a twelve-year-old boy, then it was insufficiently cryptic for his convoluted mind. He waited nearly a minute and sighed, not through impatience, but quite the opposite, relief that I was still confused.

"Victorian writers and poets," he declared and pointed to the chair that stood by the desk. He began silently reading my essay.

I sat down and wondered if he would know I had stolen the storyline from a television programme. I hadn't of course. My story was a composite of several OSS episodes. In a way, I was rather hoping he would challenge its authenticity and then I would be in a position to cross examine him on its realism. Would he have parachuted into the woods, or onto the beach? Now, I would find out how knowledgeable Captain Trevelyan was in respect of parachuting in behind enemy lines.

"Of course," he said after a long delay, "I am only here to comment on matters of grammar, spelling, punctuation and, perhaps composition."

"What about the merits of the story?"

"You are twelve years old. I am not expecting Thomas Hardy. Oliver Hardy, maybe."

A wry smile appeared on his face. He obviously liked his own jokes.

He took out a red pen and began scribbling on the page.

I told him our new guest had arrived already.

"He almost caught my mother out."

"A difficult thing to do, I imagine," he answered as wryly as his smile.

"His name is Avram," I replied, deliberately not answering the point about my mother.

"Kaleb Ben Avram?" he asked, as if he knew the answer, because there was only one Kaleb Ben Avram who would visit Berck. He then described the man in detail as if he was looking at him right now. "Medium height, dressed in a long, thigh-length black jacket and hat, with his black hair in ringlets, like Shirley Temple."

I nodded and wanted to tell him how accurate his description was. I also wanted to tell him that he was an orthodox Jew, but kept quiet, because I wasn't sure my grandmother was right about that. Surely their dress, the way they looked, made them unorthodox.

"He lost no time," the Captain added, before telling me that the man normally stayed in one of the hotels in the town when he visited Berck. "It was because the previous owners of the convent did not have any short term lets. Pity," he added. "I should have seen this coming."

The Captain spoke quite openly and yet hid his true feelings well. I imagine he would be a very good card player and could even give my granny a reasonable game of Ludo. But I knew he was troubled by our latest arrival, so I conjured up something to galvanise his constrained emotions. I knew I could jab him with a sentence that would provoke some action from him. I paused for a moment and then fired the arrow.

"He has already written something in the visitors' journal."

He looked up from the exercise book immediately and asked me to fetch it.

"What?" I asked tauntingly, for I knew exactly what he was referring to.

"The book, the book," he blurted, as if he couldn't get the words out quick enough.

I stood up and looked at the volumes of written words that lined the room.

"Which one?"

I saw the look in his face as he realised I was tormenting him and I knew I could not prolong the agony any longer.

"Oh, the journal," I said, and headed downstairs before he exploded.

As I walked up the stairs, I read the entry. It was just four lines and yet four lines that I could not understand, nor could I see the relevance of the entry.

Deep in the shady sadness of a vale
far sunken from the healthy breath of morn,
far from the fiery noon, and eve's one star,
sat gray-haired Saturn, quiet as a stone....

Trevelyan took the book from me and mouthed the words silently to himself.

"Keats," he said. "Crude and artless."

"Keats?" I replied, surprised at Trevelyan's condemnation of the same poet he had applauded previously. "But you said that Keats was the greatest of poets."

"No," he answered. "Not Keats - Avram. The man is not very subtle at all. Crude and artless," he repeated in case I hadn't fully understood that he was referring to our new visitor.

"He certainly arrived very early," I added.

The Captain mouthed a comment about the early bird catching the worm, and then told me that Kaleb Ben Avram was a Jewish Nazi hunter who was well known to the townsfolk of Berck, including von Tench and himself. Avram had visited Berck over the years, he told me, but normally stayed in one of the hotels on the front. I chose not to tell Trevelyan that Veronique had already told me what Avram's occupation was.

"Who is he looking for?" I asked, assuming all hunters were seeking a prey.

"He isn't seeking anyone," the Captain answered a little cryptically. "He thinks he has found who he is looking for and he is now looking for the evidence to prove it."

"Who is it?"

The Captain was a little reluctant to continue, but he had started the conversation and it would be more difficult to stop it abruptly than to answer my question. But his tone was all about playing the matter down.

"He is looking for a man named Ludwig who served the Nazis at a concentration camp in a town called Dachau. And he thinks von Tench is that same man."

"Which he isn't," I replied with a hint of a question in the tone of my voice.

"How many Germans do you think were named Ludwig in 1940?" He paused for just two seconds, because he didn't expect me to respond. "Thousands," he added, answering his own question. "The man is a paranoid tyrant, travelling the world looking for people with past sins that he can expose to the masses and seek retribution through the War Crime trials.

"Where is Dachau?" I asked the Captain, although I think he had forgotten he had mentioned the place.

"Just outside Munich." The answer came reluctantly and matter-of-fact, as if the location of the town was of no interest whatsoever. He shuffled across to the bookshelf. It was the first time I noticed his limp; it was subtle, but he definitely had an injury to his right leg, or perhaps his left as it was difficult to tell which. He reached up and removed a book of poems by Keats and found the one he was looking for. He handed the open book to me, asked me to read it, and sat down.

"Deep in the shady sadness of a vale, far sunken from the healthy breath of morn, far from the fiery noon, and eve's one star, sat gray-haired Saturn, quiet as a stone." I looked up to seek confirmation that I was reading the right text.

"Why have you stopped?" the Captain asked, "for the story is yet to unfold."

"Along the margin-sand..." I continued, but I stopped to ask who Saturn was.

His head was in his hands, listening to the words, as if looking for some cipher in its meaning. He jerked upwards at the sound of Saturn's name.

"He was a Roman god," he answered a little reluctantly and then told me to leave the poetry book on the table for he wanted to look at it later. I am sure he felt uneasy, culpable even, for involving me in some subterranean plot. His eyes returned to my exercise book and he began correcting my work.

"Plurals do not require an apostrophe," he commented and wrote something to this effect in the margin. "Its and it's are not the same. The first is possessive and indicates that something belongs to someone and the other is an abridged version of 'it is.'"

He made another scribble in the margin and told me that all sentences require a subject and a verb; somebody always does something. He spoke the last four words as if he was resigning himself to some great, and very irritating truth. Somebody always does something.

"Somebody always does something," he repeated and I sensed that he was talking about Mr Avram. Someone is always interfering is what he meant; why can't people just leave me alone? This is what he actually intended to say.

His eyes were on the page, but his mind was somewhere else. He snapped out of it and glanced back at the exercise book.

"This sentence about the airplane is followed by another saying 'it's propellers roared loudly', with an apostrophe that is superfluous to requirements. The easiest way to remember the rule is that a proper noun always has an apostrophe when it describes the ownership of something, such as the airplane's propellers, but when it becomes the pronoun it, the word its does not require an apostrophe. This is to avoid confusion with the shortened version of it's, meaning it is. The only time it's has an apostrophe is when it is used as this shortened version of it is."

He sounded a little annoyed but I knew that his annoyance wasn't anything to do with my poor English punctuation. This was entirely to do with our new guest.

I nodded, but he insisted I gave him a few examples to show I understood the rule. He then went on to provide explanations for the other two recurring errors in my essay. I filed these away because I wanted to change the subject back to the cryptic message that Mr Avram had left in the journal.

"What does it mean in the poem, when the writer mentions the margin-sand? What is margin-sand?"

He told me that English language and English literature are two different subjects because we cannot always rely on the writer to comply with the correct rules. I went to say 'but' and he interrupted me.

"Keats is just describing a beach, I think. You know what a margin is, don't you?"

I confirmed that I did and made a reference about the margin in my exercise book.

"Yes, but the margin is neither part of the page, nor part of the binding. It is that gap between one thing and another. So Keats is referring to the margin between the land and the sea; the beach does not belong to either because it is occupied by both elements at different times, so he calls it the margin-sand. When the tide is out the sand belongs to the land and when it is in, it belongs to the sea."

"And that is where Keats finds the Roman god Saturn?"

"Keats wrote about Saturn, he did not find the god himself."

"Who finds the god on the margin-sand then?"

"Thea finds him there. Saturn and Thea were technically not gods, but Titans. The Titans were all born of the sky and the earth, as Saturn and Thea were. The Titans were the first mythological beings, created when the universe was formed."

I went to ask another question, but he stopped me.

"This is an English language lesson, not Greek mythology."

He still seemed angry about something.

My exercise book was returned and I was asked to write two pages of sentences demonstrating that I fully understood the three common errors in my essay.

"And what did you think of the story," I asked, hoping to retrieve some comment on the content, rather than the style. But he knew what my motive was. I put my cards on the table.

"The woods or the beach?" I asked.

"Parachuting at night is not a precise art," he replied and I waited for him to add something. Seconds elapsed, before he did eventually comment further, but only to finish his sentence. "... I would imagine, Peter."

I was convinced that he thought he had already said too much. He probably regretted commenting so openly about his past life to a twelve-year-old boy. He was still encumbered by a prejudice towards children, unlike Veronique, who was happy to hold a mature conversation with me and end it with no regrets.

At the end of the lesson, I was given the journal and told to replace it in the hall. As we sat eating a cheese sandwich, Mum checked my exercise book and I complained that the content of my sandwich was not cheddar, trying to distract her from the amount of red ink on the page. She ignored my comment, or was perhaps too engrossed in my plagiarised version of a TV series. I had to distract her before she grasped the full extent of my lack of originality.

What did Dad do?" I asked, recalling the Captain's implied derision of me for not knowing his occupation. My mother almost jumped, as if she had received an electric shock.

"He didn't do anything!" she declared, dropping the exercise book on the kitchen table.

"No, I mean, what did he work at? What was his job?"

She seemed strangely relieved at this clarification of my question.

"He was apprenticed to a lock maker in London," she answered a little hesitantly, calling on her undoubted imaginative powers.

"Yes, I remember he told me that's what he did when he left school," I answered. "Was he doing that all his life then?"

What followed sounded very much like another version of the truth. Of course, he wasn't with the same employer, but that was his profession, she told me. It was a lengthy explanation with little substance, but locks, it seems, were the basis of his employment, though quite how the company he worked for secured an important contract to supply and fit all the locks on a bullring in Barcelona, was never really explained adequately in my view.

"It's a bit hot in the courtyard at this time of day," Mum commented, in what seemed like a poor attempt to change the subject. "Why don't you take Gretel for a walk to the beach? Perhaps call in to see Madame Fournier again to see if she is feeling any better today."

Gretel jumped to her feet at the word 'walk', suggesting that she had, indeed, learned English a lot quicker than I was learning French. I agreed, thinking the walk would give me time to create some sentences for my homework, all based on parachuting behind enemy lines, if I could manage it. By the time I arrived at the green door in the Rue de la Plage, I hadn't thought at all about my homework, producing instead questions for Madame Fournier about the new guest at the convent.

The rumbling noise from Veronique's stomach became apparent as soon as she turned the radio off. She winced as she sat back down in the armchair and I asked if she was feeling any better. She said she was much improved. It was definitely another version of the truth, the type I concluded that women specialised in telling. I reminded Veronique that she had previously promised to tell me about the new arrival at the guest house, Kaleb Ben Avram, the Jewish Nazi hunter who travelled the world to root out German war criminals and bring them to justice.

"Did I?" she asked and she sounded like she had completely forgotten her promise.

"You said you would tell me more of him when I next visited you."

She looked at me a little suspiciously.

"You said that it is important that I learned about this man, Kaleb Ben Avram."

Whether it was the obvious pain she was suffering from, or just forgetfulness, I am not sure, but she did eventually remember our earlier conversation. She described Avram as a young man and I suppose he is, compared to Veronique, because he was probably only half her age. This man was a fanatical German war crimes investigator, she told me, whose work was paid for by wealthy Jews who sought vengeance for the horrific acts of their tormentors. Avram believed that Ludwig von Tench had been, at least during the early years of the war, an officer based at Dachau concentration camp. The only evidence he had of this, was that both he and the guard were named Ludwig, and the guard held the rank of leutnant, the same as von Tench. Everything else, according to Veronique, was supposition on the part of Avram.

"But von Tench was from Munich," she said, as if it had relevance.

"And Munich is near Dachau," I added.

She looked a little surprised at my knowledge of German geography.

"It was something that Captain Trevelyan said," I replied, answering her questioning look.

I told her that the Captain believed that Avram had stopped looking for the Dachau officer because he believed he had already found him in von Tench.

"If he could prove it, he would have done so by now," Veronique replied. "He has visited Berck many times in recent years and has been unable to find anything to implicate Ludwig von Tench."

"Why is he unable to find proof?"

"Have you any idea how much documentation was destroyed in the war. Germany was devastated by allied bombing. Those personnel records that the Nazis did not burn themselves were destroyed by the blanket bombing of the major cities. Very little personnel records remained for the war crimes investigators."

She spoke at length about von Tench and affirmed her own belief that Avram was probably correct in his suspicions. Von Tench had not arrived in Berck until 1943, he was originally from Munich, so could easily have served at Dachau, and he was sent to the front line like many other younger soldiers and officers as the war went on. At that time, the priorities were changing, the older soldiers were removed from the front and given the more mundane jobs of watching over POWs and putting political prisoners, Jehovah's Witnesses, Jews and homosexuals on to the buses to be taken to the camps.

"Is that what this Ludwig did then, put people onto buses?"

"Apparently, according to Avram."

"And that's a war crime?"

The old woman hesitated to answer my question.

"You are too young Peter, this was long before your time. What happened to these people was horrific, beyond your imagination."

Avram had taken photographs of von Tench and shown them to victims of the Dachau concentration camp. The responses he received were not conclusive but, if he ignored those who said it was not him and the others who said they were unsure, Avram would still be left with a reasonable number of witnesses who were prepared to testify that Ludwig von Tench was the man.

"Could Ludwig not call the others as witnesses?"

She looked at me quizzically.

"The people who said he was not the war criminal," I explained.

"He would need to find them first. Anyway, it probably was him."

"But, if Avram cannot prove it, why does he keep returning to Berck."

"There are other offences that von Tench may be guilty of and Avram will not mind which of those crimes takes his suspect to the gallows. You may as well be hung for a sheep as for a lamb."

"Is it something to do with Saturn?" I asked and she winced at the pain in her stomach.

I told her about the visitors' journal and the entry that Avram had made in it. She sat pondering the matter before getting up to make us a cup of tea. When she returned to the room, she sat down and told me all about Ludwig von Tench or, at least, all she knew of him since his arrival in Berck.

There was an active group of French resistance fighters in Berck during the war. Allied planes regularly flew across to mainland Europe through the skies, directly above the small coastal town. Any information about enemy activity along that coast was of great interest to the British Intelligence Service, so it was important to maintain the resistance group in this area. However, the Germans knew this and so it was a constant battle of wits between the Nazis and the British, with the resistance fighters caught in the middle. In spite of the danger, those men and women too, provided important information to the allies. Of course, in other parts of France, the resistance were blowing up bridges, dams, factories and road and rail lines of strategic importance. But that was not the priority here in Berck. Here, along the coast, information had more value than a bridge or stretch of railway line.

The enormous contribution of the Berck resistance took a greater emphasis in the months leading up to D-Day in 1944, she told me. And it was in those nervous days of unrest that Saturn emerged. Nobody knew every member of the resistance, but there were about ten or twelve core members who lived under Nazi rule in Berck, and risked their lives to overturn the occupation of their town.

Veronique told me that Laurent, her eldest son, who was killed in the allied bombing raid, had been a member of the resistance and he had told his brother Bruno that the group had a traitor in its midst, who was passing information on to the local Gestapo. Laurent even learned the traitor's German code name, which was Saturn.

"Some believed that Ludwig von Tench was that spy," Veronique said.

"But he was a German officer, how could he be a spy?"

"Well, because he was a spy," she replied. "He had turned against the Nazi cause and was operating as a spy for the resistance, giving us information which we passed on to the British."

"So, you think he could have been a double agent then?"

She shrugged her shoulders.

"Wasn't he a rather obvious suspect?"

"Fabrice used the expression 'hiding in plain sight'."

"Fabrice the butcher?" I asked.

She nodded and I asked her if he was also a member of the resistance. Veronique laughed out loud and held her stomach, which grumbled loudly. Apparently Fabrice Dubois was not a member of the resistance. In fact, she told me, he might have been the spy himself, for even though he was not part of the group, he was a trusted friend and knew as much of what was going on as any resistance member knew. But he was an outsider, arriving in Berck just before the war began.

"So," I asked, "Saturn could have been either the butcher, Fabrice Dubois, or Ludwig von Tench?"

Veronique laughed again, only suppressing it this time in order to avoid any unnecessary pain. She tried to make herself more comfortable in the chair but whichever way she sat, the pain never seemed to leave her stomach.

"Saturn could have been anyone," she answered loudly, waving her arms as much as she could without provoking the pain. "It could just have easily been your Captain Trevelyan. After all, I saw him myself, when he was carried into the hospital on a stretcher. He was conscious then and the Germans may well have interrogated him already, even before he was operated on. The only visible wound was the bullet in his right shoulder. The Gestapo had not injured him in any other way, and very few people are fortunate enough to escape interrogation by the Gestapo unharmed."

"If he was shot in the shoulder, why was he on a stretcher?" I asked her.

"Have you ever been shot?" she asked. "You cannot walk."

Gretel jumped up at the word walk and began scampering around my feet. I desperately wanted to ask Veronique how Captain Trevelyan could possibly be the spy Saturn but, by the time I stopped Gretel jumping up at me, Veronique was on her feet and opening the front door for me.

"I'll come back to see you soon, Madame Fournier."

"Veronique," she answered. "I prefer Veronique."

As I went to leave, she called me back. "You are a very good listener, Peter."

"Perry Mason says that listening is one of the best exercises we can do."

12

When I was born, my dad must have been around thirty years old, so I am not qualified to speak of his early life, except through hearsay and speculation. But, in the same way that I didn't know him for the whole of his life, he didn't know me for the entirety of mine either. I have the impression that he was not around much when I was a baby and Mum had to raise me without his help. That isn't a criticism of him, as I don't suppose many dads took a direct involvement in changing nappies and feeding baby.

What is important, I suppose, in these arbitrary recollections is that he was there when I was born and I was there when he died. In reality I knew him for just twelve years. If you discard the days of my infancy, we were together for less than eight years. And, during that time, he went missing for a two-year period. So, maybe we knew each other for five or six years. I knew Terry Williams longer than that and I wouldn't say we were particularly close, well not enough for him to send out a search party for me I imagine.

And yet, five or six years seems to be plenty of time to get to know somebody, but then my father didn't talk much. That, in itself, wouldn't necessarily be a problem but, unfortunately neither did I. In truth I can't remember a single occasion when we sat down and chatted. Even when he took me to Upton Park to watch a football match, it was all irrelevant chatter about the team.

Whenever I stop to empty my mind or, at least try to clear all the thoughts from my head, so that my brain might just idle for a moment, the sound of what I remember him saying the most echoes in that tiny space between now and the now to come. "Where's the little bloke," he would ask when he stepped through the front door, home from a day's work.

Locksmiths don't sweat as much as some other professions, like a coalminer. A coalminer's sweat-sodden body is stained by the black marks of his trade, that sit upon the surface of the skin differently, as if they are part of that skin, like the fine hairs along his sinewy arms. The evidence of his hard labour is obvious to all, the unquestionable proof of a sooty face and gritty hands.

I never got the impression that my dad worked hard in the same sense as a coalminer. My mum may not have had a paying job, yet her single most important duty in life was to know, at any given moment in time, where the little bloke was. I wondered why I was the first thing on his mind when he came back from work. Why wasn't it Mum, because she loved him more than I did. And yet, that relationship was going on around me for twelve years and I didn't really notice it. I never realised that my mother loved my dad so much until he died.

In the same way, I had not realised until Veronique had told me, that through the long dark years of the war, the people of Berck had watched that same war pass over their heads as first German aircraft bombing England headed north and then later, when the Allied forces crossed the channel, flying south to bomb the French airfields, including the one just outside Berck. They could not know, of course, that those raids were the precursor to D-day, or perhaps some of them did, for this was the time of the resistance, when the agent Saturn was at large. It would have been his objective to uncover such information for his Gestapo bosses.

In the sky above the courtyard garden, I never saw any aircraft pass overhead, just the occasional giant black cormorant that wandered inland from the long coastline that provided its food. It stopped once, on the roof, looking like some long extinct Pterodactylus. It was there, that Tuesday morning when I ran inside to tell my mother, but remembered she had rushed off into town before I had finished my toast, promising to be home in time for lunch. If she was late, there was a packet of biscuits in the cupboard, she said, that would tide me over until she got back.

I wasn't sure whether our temporary guest was in his room, but presumed he may have been because there was no entry in the visitors' journal and I had not heard anyone leave the house.

In mother's absence, I took my tea and toast out into the shaded courtyard, picking up along the way, the estate agent's information sheet about the house. I remembered there was a diagram on one side, outlining the layout of the building. The structure was difficult to come to terms with by just simply walking around it and the diagram helped.

123

The house couldn't really be described as a maze, but it had the same qualities. The dog-leg passageway was duplicated on the ground floor and basement levels, but not on the first floor or attic level. The ground floor was slightly raised from ground level; you had to walk up steps to the front door and, at the rear of the property, there were steps down into the courtyard garden. More steps at both the front and rear of the house led down into a subterranean light well that provided a degree of natural brightness into a basement. It served another purpose at the front of the house, where coal could be delivered through a manhole in the pavement to an underground coal cellar. I have heard this called a light hole, or an area, or more commonly, in London, as an aerie. At one end of the downstairs aerie was a room which was attached to the house but not in the house. It was a margin-room and Mum said it used to be an outside privy, but it was now used as a storage room, for brooms and brushes.

I examined the plan of the house. Back in England, it would have been described as a Victorian or Regency house, but I don't suppose those expressions count for very much in France. The basement level lost that title very quickly and from the first day was simply referred to as downstairs. It had a tiny lobby area off the front aerie which led to the dog-leg passageway. Along this, there was a living room at the front of the building and a large kitchen at the rear. This really was a substantial size room that was obviously used as a kitchen and dining area for the nuns who used to live there and, perhaps even the monks before them; although it probably didn't have plastered walls and tiled floors in those days. On the other side of the passageway was my mother's bedroom and a bathroom.

On the ground floor, above the basement kitchen and living room, there were two more bedrooms, one used by me and the other by our temporary guests. On the opposite side of the crooked passageway was a smaller spare room, which mother intended to use for sewing and perhaps as a reading room in the winter, and there was another bathroom, which was reserved for the temporary guests. I was instructed by mother to use the basement bathroom.

The first floor level, occupied by Captain Trevelyan, was smaller than the ground floor, but larger than the attic level above. Trevelyan had a large landing area, a living room, a bedroom and a bathroom. Ludwig von Tench had the same rooms, but these were designed with smaller proportions.

Through the house ran a wide set of stairs, with a short landing on each dog-leg section, which enabled you to pause and catch your breath, for the steps were quite steep. The stairs were wider than we had in our old house in London; not as wide as a stately home I had seen on holiday in Norfolk, but wide enough for two people to pass easily on the stairs.

The courtyard garden was the same level as the street to the front of the building – slightly lower than the ground floor and a few steps down into the basement. The document described it as being on the mezzanine level.

I finished my tea and toast and made sure that Gretel had enough water before going upstairs. I made sure to close the kitchen door, as my mum had told me, to prevent Gretel running around the house. The puppy had calmed down quite a lot since the day she arrived and she had access to the garden if she wanted to go outside.

"Did you know that Madame Fournier had a second son who was killed in the war?" I asked the German in the attic, as soon as I had wished him bonjour.

"Yes," answered von Tench. "And she has a daughter also, who joined the silent order of Franciscan nuns who lived in this very convent. In those days, the rooms were called cells and the sisters lived a sheltered life, configured in order that each young woman might nourish their own deep relationship with God. Only solitude, they believed, could introduce them to the divine joy which silent devotion may bring."

The old man told me that the young woman, who was Bruno's older sister, was named Edith, but she became Sister Marie-Claire when she joined the order during the war. She went to Italy around the time of the allied invasion, soon after the Gestapo decided to commandeer the convent for the use of their officers. According to von Tench, Edith was still alive apparently, and living in Rome.

"This building was sold by the Catholic church many years ago," he added.

Veronique must have been either very proud of her daughter for adopting a life of penance, or very sad, and disappointed, perhaps, that she was wasting her life cooped up in a tiny cell praying to God all the time. The information about Edith, which von Tench volunteered with some prompting from me, made sense of the photo I had seen in Madame Fournier's living room, of the three children. The two boys and one girl were, almost certainly, Veronique's children, Laurent and Edith, and Bruno, who was several years younger than them. But why, I wondered, had Veronique not told me about her daughter? Why would she wish to keep this secret?

"Why did she become a nun?" I asked as I handed him my French homework.

"I cannot remember," replied von Tench. "She was in her early twenties and she had boyfriends, including a German soldier, I think. Perhaps he died, I don't recall."

I walked around the room, which, despite being smaller than the Captain's room, looked surprisingly larger, probably because it wasn't lined with books. The view from the attic window was of the rooftops to the rear of the building. It was impossible to see down into the courtyard garden and it faced the wrong direction to enjoy a view of the sea. The paint on the wooden window frames was cracked and the lock on the window was broken, not that anyone could possibly climb up that far.

As I waited for his comments on my work, I noticed the small nails that punctured the window frame at intervals, but provided a securing point for nothing that I could see. I then realised that von Tench must have, at some time in the past, pinned his radio aerial around the window frame as the Captain had done.

"Do you have a radio?" I asked.

"No, but I sometimes listen to Captain Trevelyan's radio."

He took a red pen and began correcting my work.

"I visited Madame Fournier yesterday," I said, making what appeared to be small talk, but which was, in fact, more significant than that. Perry Mason often used this strategy to lure his witnesses into a false sense of security.

Von Tench mumbled a response, so I continued by telling him what she had told me, or some of it.

"She was telling me about the resistance in the war, and about the agent named Saturn."

He didn't react as I imagined he would.

"Saturn," I repeated, in case he hadn't heard it.

But, he failed to look up from my homework and mumbled something about why on earth would she do that? Why? Wasn't that obvious? Because of the arrival of Kaleb Ben Avram, I answered expecting him to look up. But he didn't. His lack of a reaction proved that he was either perfectly qualified to be a double agent, or entirely innocent of that allegation.

"I am sure the Captain has warned you about Madame Fournier, Peter," he replied. "You must not give too much credibility to anything she says."

Are they lies, I wondered, or just another version of the truth? I disregarded the idea. Instead I told him that Veronique did not necessarily believe that he was Saturn.

"The German spy Saturn," I added, as if there was another person of the same name.

"That's very decent of her," he commented sardonically.

"She said that Saturn could just as easily be the butcher, Fabrice Dubois."

"Yes," he answered a little tiredly. "And Saturn could be her son, the baker, Bruno Fournier, but I don't suppose she suggested that to you, did she?"

I didn't have time to answer before he indicated that I should sit down, in order that we could begin the lesson.

I was distracted throughout the class, not just because I was unable to concentrate on anything other than the spy Saturn, but more significantly from the incessant, albeit muted sound of Gretel barking. She could get between the basement and the courtyard and I had made sure she had plenty of water to drink. But she wasn't used to being on her own for long periods. I wasn't sure why Mum hadn't taken the puppy out with her and Gretel was probably fretting about our absence.

By the time the lesson ended, all I could remember was how to tell someone that my aunt's pen was on the table, but as I didn't have an aunt, I wasn't sure how useful the lesson had been.

"There is no rush to end the lesson," I told von Tench. "My mother is probably still out shopping. She said she may be late."

"Well then you can make a start on translating the English sentences in your homework book into French. And you better attend to your puppy too, or the neighbours will be complaining about her barking."

I nodded and went, a little reluctantly, to leave.

"Did you ever have a radio?" I asked.

"No," he answered a little impatiently, and I went downstairs, stopping on the landing to listen at the door, hoping to determine whether the Captain was in his room. All was silent, so I continued down the stairs to the ground floor. I wanted to look at the journal, but there was continuous barking coming from the basement. The yelping and whining sounded strangely muffled, and I wondered if Gretel had got herself shut in the kitchen. I decided to check for the latest journal entry anyway, ignoring Gretel, who had probably run for shelter after catching a sight of that giant cormorant that had been loitering on the roof.

13

There was a partial entry in the book. It ended abruptly, the sentence unfinished, as if our guest had been disturbed.

> *Along the margin-sand large foot-marks went,*
> *no further than to where his feet had strayed,*
> *and slept there since*

The words did not make sense until I realised that they were a continuation of the previous day's entry.

Mum was obviously not home yet, otherwise she would have put a stop to the barking from the basement. I decided to go out into the courtyard and walk down the basement steps, through the rear airie, just in case Gretel was caught up somewhere. As I went, I questioned why Gretel was not lounging in her favourite and shadiest part of the garden, but not enough to suspect anything was wrong. But there was something wrong. There was something very wrong.

The kitchen had been ransacked. Gretel had been shut in the larder cupboard and every drawer in the room had been opened and emptied. At first I wondered if the giant cormorant had got in and trashed the place but, then, how did it shut the dog in the cupboard and what did it use to open the drawers with, its beak? I surveyed the room, trying to determine what could have caused all this mess. This room had not been wrecked by a trapped pigeon, or even a trapped cormorant. This room had been burgled.

Nothing appeared to be broken, but documentation, tea towels, napkins, cutlery and baking tins were strewn across the kitchen floor. Then it suddenly occurred to me that someone might still be in the house. My stomach jumped and I stood completely still for a moment, listening. I put the lead on Gretel and together we crept along the corridor and peeked in each room. It was difficult to tell whether the spare room, or the sewing room as my mum called it, had been disturbed. It was currently being used as a junk room and still contained some cardboard boxes of unpacked items from the house move. But I noticed that all of those boxes had been emptied, so the burglar had been in here.

Mum's bedroom had been ruined, although nothing had been broken or torn, just scattered about the room. There wasn't much in the bathroom to be disturbed, but the bathroom cabinet had been emptied, the door was left swinging open and, strangely, the panel on the side of the bath had been ripped off. Even the coats that had been hanging in the lobby area were heaped on the floor, with handkerchiefs and scarves trailing about the place.

I took Gretel upstairs but everything seemed to be untouched; although it was difficult to tell with my bedroom, which could only be improved by the visit of a burglar. I thought about running upstairs to find the Captain or Mr von Tench. But, instead, I decided to rush outside and find my mother. She always walked the same way home from the main shopping street of Rue Carnot, so we could not miss each other. I didn't want her to arrive home before I found her, because I didn't want her to be as frightened as I was.

I walked up past the baker's shop and looked up and down the Rue Carnot, but there was no sign of her. I was about to run home when suddenly a hand grabbed my shoulder from behind.

"What's wrong young Peter?" asked Bruno and, in that moment I didn't even notice that I had reverted to *young* Peter again. I was breathing nearly as hard as Gretel, whose tiny legs had been rushed hither and thither as we searched for my mother.

"We've been burgled!"

Bruno grabbed my hand and we walked as quickly as Gretel could manage back to the baker's shop. He flipped the *open* sign to say *closed* and slammed the door, much to the annoyance of two women coming towards the shop.

"Emergency," he shouted back to them and the word resonated in my head. My mind had been too occupied to appreciate that this was an emergency. But, now someone had described it as such, I began to shake a little. Gretel sensed something was wrong and kept looking up at me, as if she expected an explanation. I didn't have one. Bruno snatched Gretel up from the floor and carried her the rest of the way home.

By good fortune, we arrived at the corner of our street at exactly the same time as my mother, who was walking slowly in front of us. She looked slightly different and I realised she had been to the hairdresser.

"We've been burgled," I called to her and by the time I could offer an explanation, we had arrived at the door.

In her hurry, mother slammed the front door behind her and the noise roused the Captain and von Tench, who came downstairs to see what was wrong.

"We've been burgled," the pair of us declared in chorus.

Bruno put Gretel down and handed me the lead.

We walked around the basement assessing the damage, with Bruno leading the way, just in case someone was still in the house. Gretel kept looking at me and I kept looking at mother, wondering if she was going to cry. She didn't. My mum didn't cry very often; I don't even recall her crying when my dad died. Mum cared, I know that much, but she had this incredible ability to contain and control her feelings. Perhaps those particular feelings, the ones that abducted her emotions, went somewhere else. For all I know, maybe there were tiny explosions taking place all over her body; but nothing ever changed her countenance. Perry Mason would have difficulty cross examining my mother.

"Had I better call the police?" asked mother in a resigned tone of voice.

"There's no need," Bruno replied.

As he spoke, a variety of expressions appeared on the other five faces. Mum fashioned a questioning look because she did not understand Bruno's last statement. I thought it sounded as if he knew who was responsible, so my expression was not too dissimilar. The Captain sighed, as if the past had revisited his soul and von Tench pursed his mouth, as if something terrible was about to happen. Gretel simply looked up at me and back at her empty bowl that had been kicked over and the water trod across the floor of the kitchen.

"You have Kaleb Ben Avram staying here, don't you?" Bruno asked mother.

Somehow, my mum understood his meaning.

"My guest did this? Why? Why would he do this?"

Bruno explained that Avram was a Nazi war criminal investigator who visited Berck regularly. He normally stayed in one of the beachfront hotels, but Bruno was certain he had always held a desire to stay here at the old convent, but the previous owners had only ever accommodated long-term guests.

"Why would he want to stay here?" she asked.

"This building was occupied by the Gestapo during the war. Avram has longed for the opportunity to look around this place."

"Who is he looking for?"

"He isn't looking for anyone," answered von Tench a little wearily. "He has found who he is looking for and now he is simply looking for evidence to support his wild theories."

The German told my mother that Avram believes he served at the Dachau concentration camp during the war.

"He also believes that I am the spy referred to by locals in Berck as Saturn. He believes that I am responsible for the deaths of five resistance fighters who were executed by the Gestapo in 1944."

My mother thanked Bruno for his help and said she would speak with Mr Avram when he returned. Bruno left, but not before asking mother to let him know later how she

135

was. The two old men returned to their rooms and I was instructed to sit in the courtyard. Mysteriously, my mother made no attempt to tidy the rooms up.

Later, when she heard Avram arrive upstairs, Mum asked him to accompany her to the basement, where she showed him the devastation. I sat in the courtyard, out of sight, but close enough to hear what was said.

He denied it was him, of course, saying he had been out all morning. But mother didn't accept his explanation.

"You will have to leave Mr Avram," she told him. "I realise that you need to find alternative accommodation, but you must leave on Thursday. Whatever has gone on here, I don't want my family to be part of it. Do you understand?"

He nodded his head, but challenged the decision once more.

Sometimes, people reveal a lot more by how they say something than by what they actually say. This happens often in Perry Mason, when he is cross examining a witness. And it happened this day too, even though Kaleb Ben Avram wasn't under cross examination.

"Do you have any children?" my mother asked him, when he offered up his last appeal against her decision.

"Yes, I have three in total," he answered.

"Then you will know why I have to make this decision. I will not let anything hurt my son. You may, or may not be responsible for what has happened here today, but I will not take chances with my son's life."

What occurred to me, sitting in that quiet courtyard, was not his actual reply, but the structure of his answer. Why would anyone express the number of children they had in that obtuse way? Unless, of course, you have been married more than once. So, I concluded this was what he meant.

I wanted, so much, to cross examine him at that moment. Was it he, or his wife, who transgressed? That would tell me a lot about the man. Can you trust anyone who cannot be trusted by his own wife? 'I have three in total' he had said, instead of simply 'three'.

Of course, a man of with his background understood my mother's position, and yet he continued to deny any responsibility for the act of vandalism. But she had made her mind up. He had to leave on Thursday.

"May I just say something, Mrs Jackson?" he asked as he walked towards the door to go upstairs. She looked directly at him and waited for him to speak.

"It is true, that I have searched many properties looking for evidence of Nazi criminals. So this scene is not unfamiliar to me. What I can tell you, if it is of any use to you, is that, whoever did carry out this search, did not find what they were looking for. This person is not half way through a search; he or she has completely finished the search and found nothing."

Mother remained silent, waiting for further clarification.

"Every part of the basement," he explained, "has been scoured. If this person had found what they were looking for, they would have stopped searching and left. This person did not find what they were looking for." He paused for a moment. "If this information is of any help to you, then I am pleased; but then, this is just my professional opinion."

His words convinced me that he had not burgled our home. But, if it was not him, then what was the real burglar looking for?   What did my mother have that would cause someone to reek this havoc?   I could not believe that what the person was actually looking for was some remnant of the previous occupants, the nuns or the Gestapo.

14

I don't believe in time and space. Well, I believe in space, because it is there, that's undeniable. But I don't believe in time, a concept which strikes me as something invented by man to serve his own purposes. Surely it should be change and space, not time and space, because it is the changes that count, not the time it takes for those changes to occur.

Every second of every day, trillions of things change. Things are created or die, grow or shrink, rise, succeed or fall, and measuring how long it takes for those things to happen has little to do with the process in my view.

As proof of time's irrelevance, someone suggested in parliament, just before we left England, that time should be adjusted by one hour twice a year. And why? Apparently because some politician was incensed at the waste of useful daylight hours during the summer. I rest my case, m'lord, because how can something as important as time be changed to suit man's purposes?

Space exists, the exploits of Yuri Gagarin, Alan Shepard and Valentina Teroshkova are living proof of that. And now the Americans are planning to send a space ship to fly around Mars. So I accept that space exists. But time is a human concept, manufactured for man's own purposes.

If I needed proof of this theory, then I just needed to look around our flat after the intruder had broken in. The contents of every room had been moved, lots of things had changed. It was the change that mattered, not the time it had taken for that change to happen.

Perhaps it was just the way I was feeling about being exiled in France, but change was becoming public enemy number one because everything had changed since we left our home in England, well almost everything. At first, time was important because my concern was how long would it take for my life to return to normal. Then I realised that *normal* was living in London, not some provincial town in another country.

It was change that mattered, not time because change was having a greater influence on my life than time and space put together. I needed to change my life here in France by restoring as much of my previous life as was possible; that was the solution to my problem.

I was considering where to start when Mum told me to help clear up the basement rooms. It took a couple of hours, which was probably twice as long as it took the intruder to make the mess in the first place. What did that tell us about time?

When we finally sat down, it was Mum's perception of change that confirmed my theory. My mother was convinced that a French loaf did not last as long as the bread back home, although I am not sure what difference it made because we bought a fresh loaf every day anyway. It wasn't just that French loaves were inferior to British bread, although that was true. But French loaves changed more quickly, deteriorated more rapidly. I was pleased that Mum shared my view about time and change.

The morning after the burglary, which wasn't a burglary because nothing was stolen, I offered to walk to the baker's shop to get some bread, but Mum insisted I stayed at home. I sensed she was still nervous about the events of the previous day and felt that by keeping me in, she would be keeping me safe. The rooms may have been tidied up and all our possessions had been put back where they belonged, but something was still troubling my mother. Perhaps she, like me, didn't believe Kaleb Ben Avram was responsible for what happened and, if that was the case, then who did ransack our apartment? What were they looking for? And, more importantly to my mother, was I in any danger if the intruder decided to return?

Mother examined the bread we had left over from yesterday, smelled it, prodded it and declared it inedible, even for toasting. In the absence of toast, we had scrambled eggs for breakfast and we ate them in the courtyard, where mother had set up a small table for that purpose.

It was a bright, sunny day and the position of the house meant that there was always one part of the enclosure that remained in the shade. Mum liked sitting in the sun, but I preferred the shade. So we found a spot that accommodated both our preferences.

Whilst there were no English language newspapers in Berck, my mum must still have had some access to news from home because, whenever we sat like this, she would

141

tell me about things that had happened back home. It was her, in fact, who told me about the discussions at home regarding changing the clocks twice each year. I tried to explain my theory to her but I'm not sure she grasped its principles. All she was worried about was how the little birds would cope with us changing the clocks in the spring and autumn.

"I don't think they would know that the clocks had been changed," I told Mum, but I don't think she understood.

Gretel was beginning to get anxious. She was a creature of habit and wanted to go for her morning walk.

I reminded Mum that, if I was not allowed out, she would need to take Gretel for a walk, but she told me I could do it later. I wondered how she managed to convince herself that it would somehow be safer for me to go outdoors later that day. What did she know that I didn't? It was inconceivable that the police would have apprehended the offender, because there had been no sign of my mother actually informing the police of the crime.

Mother dropped yesterday's loaf into the bin. It clanged and startled the now dozing Gretel.

"Once you have finished your lesson with Captain Trevelyan, you can pop round to the bakery to get some bread so we can have sandwiches for lunch."

"But the lesson doesn't finish until twelve."

"Then it will be a late lunch, Peter."

I was as much a creature of habit as Gretel and I wanted to remind Mum that lunch was always at twelve o'clock. However, I kept quiet and just added this fact to the growing list of things that were subject to change now we lived in France.

One thing was certain, she was determined to prevent me leaving the house that morning.

"What about Gretel?" I asked. "She needs her exercise."

"Okay," she conceded. "I will walk Gretel today."

As I passed by the hallway on the ground floor, on my way upstairs, I couldn't resist looking at the visitors' journal, even though I was sure that the departing Kaleb Ben Avram would not have written anything in it. Why would he bother? I was wrong; there were more lines about Saturn.

.......upon the sodden ground
his old right hand lay nerveless, listless, dead,
unsceptred; and his realmless eyes were closed;
while his bowed head seemed listening to the Earth,

Trevelyan normally had his head buried in a book when I arrived, but this morning he seemed to be anxious, awaiting my arrival, and he asked me immediately whether I had any news about the burglary. "I think we are now calling him an intruder, Captain," I told him. " There is nothing missing, so it doesn't really qualify as a burglary."

I anticipated his next comment because he had suddenly realised that my mum had not reported the matter to the police.

"So Mum doesn't want to report the incident."

He shook his head disapprovingly and I sensed he was thinking about taking the matter further with my mother, so I added a codicil. "But she is still very angry about it," I assured him and said she hoped it would all be forgotten when Mr Avram had left.

The Captain didn't like my response and I could see he considered the matter far from over. I wasn't sure he would consider it over, even when Avram was arrested.

Why did everyone think it was Avram who had wrecked the basement rooms? What could he have been searching for in our rooms? Surely if he thought von Tench was the person he was looking for, he would have hunted for clues in his rooms, not ours. I could not hold my tongue and said as much to the Captain.

"Ludwig von Tench is a good man, Peter. He is not the man that Avram thinks he is. And he certainly is not the spy they called Saturn."

I asked him how he could be so certain.

"Veronique Fournier," he declared.

"What about Veronique Fournier?"

"Veronique once confessed that she knew who Saturn was and, if it had been Ludwig, then she would have done something with that information, after all, she lost her husband, and her son in the war. And her daughter became a nun."

He said the last bit as if becoming a nun was at least as bad as dying.

"She knows who Saturn is?" I asked disbelievingly. "But you said I shouldn't believe anything that Veronique says."

He shrugged his shoulders and retrieved a book from the shelves.

"When did she say this?" I asked.

"A few years ago, at a New Year party."

"She probably had too much to drink."

"Peter, believe me, none of us would say such a thing, drunk or otherwise; not unless it was true."

She has never said who it was, of course, which led the Captain to one conclusion. The only way she would know who Saturn was, is because she was Saturn.

"Otherwise, why would she protect a German spy?"

"Because, perhaps Saturn was her son, Bruno; that could be why she would not say who the spy was."

"Well, there is one person who agrees with you." He paused, realising that he was saying too much to a young boy with a vivid imagination.

"What, Ludwig believes Bruno to be Saturn?" I asked and he looked shaken by the fact that a small boy could have noticed such a thing. It wasn't difficult to work out who he was talking about. Ludwig and the Captain must have spent many evenings discussing this matter at length. They must both have put forward their cases and reached their conclusions who Saturn was. Trevelyan believed it to be Veronique and Ludwig von Tench thought it was her son Bruno. I imagine it was easy to reach either of these conclusions because the Fournier family had lost so much at the expense of the war. There must have been many regrets for them. It would have been easy for any member of that family to have gone over to the Germans, if only to end the nightmare that threatened to overwhelm them. It was also entirely credible that Veronique herself held the secret of who Saturn really was.

In the Case of the Desperate Daughter, Delia Street told Perry that every woman was entitled to at least one secret.

'What's yours?" he asked her. 'You'll never know', she answered. That was very clever, I thought at the time. That is the essence of a secret. Once it is revealed, it loses its purpose, its identity and its power; it is no longer a secret, changed by the fact that it has been spoken of to another person.

As I hesitated, mulling over the various pieces of evidence, if indeed they even qualified as evidence, Trevelyan seized the opportunity to end the conversation and begin my geography lesson.

"Can we do some local geography?" I asked. "So I can get a sense of where I am living now? And perhaps what the area was like in the past?"

Trevelyan was not a fool; he knew where I was trying to lead him.

"What, like the woods and the beach and the aerodrome?" he asked rhetorically.

"Information from this area must have been essential for the allied bombing raids, because all the aircraft passed over this point didn't they?"

He ignored me, not giving any credence to my attempt to prise some information from him. Instead, we spent the next hour talking about continents and oceans and faraway places that were made extraordinary and exciting in an attempt to draw me away from any talk of the war. But war was about to be declared outside Trevelyan's door.

Footsteps clip-clopped up the stairs. We both stopped talking and we heard tapping on a door; not our door, but the one upstairs. The steps didn't sound like a man, but we both feared and assumed that it was Kaleb Ben Avram, grasping his opportunity of confronting von Tench. Trevelyan got up from his seat and went to walk to the door, but he stopped when he heard my mother's voice on the upstairs landing. We both listened as hard as we could.

"I have given this matter a lot of thought, Mister von Tench; I didn't sleep a wink last night worrying about it. Rightly or wrongly, Mister Avram believes you to be a war criminal and his clear intention was to use my home as a base for his enquiries into such matters. I have terminated his residence and he is leaving the building as we speak."

She hesitated, trying to remember exactly what she wanted to say. She had been awake all night and had obviously rehearsed her prepared speech over and over in her mind. "I cannot permit this situation to continue in my home, so I must ask you, invite you, to find alternative accommodation."

I looked at the Captain's face and, in that moment, I realised that my mother had no idea that von Tench and the Captain were a couple, married in all but the formalities or, more correctly, the legalities. How could she not have known this?

Trevelyan rushed to the landing and looked up the stairs.

"Mrs Jackson," he called, climbing the stairs as slowly as he spoke. I was sure he didn't know what he was going to say; he just knew he had to say something. "Mister Avram thinks Ludwig is a war criminal, he is convinced he worked at the Dachau concentration camp; he believes he is this person, this spy, Saturn that you have heard spoken of. And Avram believes all these things because he wants them to be true. But that does not make them true. There is no evidence that they are true. Ludwig may have been the spy Saturn, but then so may many others – Bruno, Veronique, Fabrice Dubois the butcher, or even myself; any one of us could well have been this person who betrayed the resistance fighters."

He stopped for a moment, to catch his breath and to consider whether he should even reveal the next piece of information. But everyone anticipated it. None of us listening to his plea thought he was finished; we all knew he was about to say something important, just like when the star witness took the stand in an episode of Perry Mason.

"Five young men were executed in the courtyard garden downstairs. Do you really believe that the man responsible for such a gruesome act could continue to live here? That he would choose to live here, if he was the person responsible for their deaths?"

Mother was shocked by this piece of information and looked down the stairs wondering how I might react to such news.

My mum turned back towards von Tench and spoke.

"Not today, or tomorrow, but soon please Mister von Tench. I refuse to bring up my son in this undercurrent of fear and suspicion."

She returned down the stairs, took my hand and led me down to the basement. I turned to look at the Captain. He knew it would be pointless to tell my mother that the lesson had not ended.

In the hallway stood Kaleb Ben Avram; he was standing there with his suitcase in his hand and had heard every word.

"Goodbye Mrs Jackson, and thank you very much for your hospitality." He spoke politely and I was surprised by the nature of his character, not that I knew much of the man, of course. But it was an oddity, a strange quality that I was not expecting to see. This was a softly spoken man who remained unruffled by whatever life threw at him. Even this arbitrary act of injustice did not seduce him to anger, nor did it even provoke him to change his mild-mannered tone. This was a persuasive man who understood immediately how his genial influence would have no effect upon the decision that had been made. Indeed, I wondered whether his quiet composure might actually enrage my mother, for I had seen before how such a calm temperament can arouse uncontrollable exasperation from the other party.

He handed her an envelope, presumably containing his rent, then smiled at me and left the house. He put up no further defence, as if he understood my mother's position completely. He had probably been in this situation many times.

Gretel practically dropped the lead at my feet when I returned to the basement and Mum gave me some money to purchase a loaf. In any other circumstance, I don't believe my mother would have allowed me to leave the house so soon after the man had been dispatched from our home. But we both knew I was in no danger from him. He worked within the close shadow of death and yet there was a passive and almost endearing quality to his personality.

I took Gretel in a different direction, sweeping right to the northern end of the town, close to where Veronique Fournier lived and headed off towards the sand dunes that I had seen previously. The road turned right, away from the sea, but a footpath ran through a rarely used car park. This led around the dunes and meandered off in the same direction as the coast. After a short walk, trees began to appear across from the beach, which was much narrower on this side of the town. The trees soon became a wood and I realised that this was the same wood that ran all the way up to the aerodrome. It was a little haven, an undiscovered place between sea and land, that same margin land that Trevelyan had spoken of. The trees thickened and the copse became a wood and the wood became a small forest, with oak, birch and chestnuts, just as we had at home. Had it not been for the ocean sweeping away out into the Atlantic, I could easily have been back in England.

This was an ideal spot for a picnic. Here and there, small clearings appeared which housed wild plants that preferred the heavy shade of the canopied forest. At home there would be bluebells and there may have been bluebells here too a few months ago. But not now, the temperature was too hot for even the bravest of plants. On the edge of the wood, in that margin land, shrubs sprung up in the sandy soil. Sea Campion, so fond of shingle and the sea salt spray, grew in abundance and a cabbage-looking plant had colonised that part of the land that stood just beyond the ocean's reach.

I imagined that this might have been the very spot where Captain Trevelyan fell to the ground back in 1944. Hidden by the woods, he would have buried his chute and made his way to the agreed meeting point. I wondered who his contact might have been.

I turned and headed back home, my head so full of imaginings. I would tell Mum about this secret place, possibly the only place in Berck where you could hear the crashing of the sea, because at the other end of town the sea was too far away to be heard.

The shop was empty when I arrived and Bruno seemed to be conducting some kind of stock check in the back room. He hadn't been there for long, however, because he had seen Avram walk passed carrying his suitcase.

"He is off to find a room at one of the hotels on the front," he commented when he heard the bell ring on the door.

"Mum told him he had to leave."

"I know. Good riddance, isn't that what you say in England."

"But I don't really believe he ransacked our home," I told him.

"Look Peter," Bruno began, as if he was about to give me a lecture on the subject of growing up. "Single-mindedness and dedication are great characteristics in a human being, but only up to the point where they become an obsession. Avram is a young Nazi hunter. In thirty years' time he will be an old Nazi hunter. In sixty years' time he will be a dead Nazi hunter, and only one thing would have changed; he would have wasted his life. If you are the same person in sixty years time as you are now Peter, then you would have wasted your life too. Forget about this Saturn business, it is in the past."

As he spoke, I was reminded of my thoughts on time and change. Perhaps it is a competition between the two.

Avram is changing slower than time itself and my own life is changing much quicker.

I told Bruno that, at school, back in England, we were told that we should not forget about the war, because only by remembering it can each generation ensure that such a tragedy does not happen again.

"You lost your father and your older brother Laurent through the war. If you forget the war, do you not forget them too? Do you not do them a disservice." I regretted the remark as soon as it left my mouth.

He could not forget his brother and father, he admitted, nor would he forget the war, but he insisted that I had no need to consider it at all, because I was not there.

"Just tell me one thing about this Saturn business," I asked.

"I cannot tell you who he...."

"or she," I interrupted.

"I cannot tell you who Saturn was."

For a moment, I wondered whether he meant cannot or would not. But I dismissed the thought.

"No, I realise that, but how did the resistance find out about the spy's existence in the first place? Who was it who found out about Saturn? Who mentioned that name first, Bruno?"

The baker thought for a moment, but relented when he could think of no good reason for withholding the information from me. Perhaps he considered I was behaving like a puppy dog myself, gnawing away, like a dog with a bone, as they say.

"My sister Edith told us." He thought about stopping there, but I just looked at him resolutely because I knew there was more he could say, perhaps even wanted to say. "Her boyfriend was a young German soldier named Dieter Weber. He was just a low ranking soldier, a Private I think, but he worked in the administrative office that supported the Gestapo officers who met with Saturn. I do not think he knew the identity of the spy but he told Edith about the traitor's existence after Laurent was killed."

"And Edith is a nun now?"

"Yes, now she is Sister Marie Claire. She lives in a Franciscan convent in the outskirts of Rome. She went there soon after the allied invasion in 1944."

"Do you see her?"

"No, the sisters are rarely released and I have never visited Rome. The nuns are allowed home for deaths in the family, very special occasions, that sort of thing."

"So, do you think Avram is wrong about von Tench then?"

"Very much so. I think he is completely wrong, and I do not accept Fabrice's view that von Tench is hiding in plain sight. I think it is more likely to be his friend than von Tench himself"

"Who, Captain Trevelyan?"

"Yes, he was the one who knew the contact name for the resistance in Berck, and it was Trevelyan who was shot and captured when he parachuted into this town, just before the landings."

He made a convincing case, but it was unlikely, in my mind, that a professional soldier like Captain Trevelyan would be the one to crack under interrogation.

"What have the police said about the burglary?" Bruno asked. "And did any of them speak English?"

"We haven't seen the police."

"What?"

"No, my mum decided not to report it. Nothing was stolen and it only took us a couple of hours to tidy the rooms up."

He adopted a commanding stance, hands on hips and casting a harsh stare towards me, as if I had any influence over my mother in such matters.

"But you must report it. Why would she not report it?"

I shrugged my shoulders. Mum had her own way of dealing with things and the most frequently employed response was to ignore any event that might upset her. It didn't surprise me that she failed to call the police. She would just see that as prolonging the agony. Get up, dust yourself off, and start all over again; that was her cheerful refrain, her motto in life.

I decided not to tell Bruno about my mum's conversation with Ludwig. I was hoping that she would have calmed down and changed her mind by the time I got home. However, there was one big problem with this plan. It was not in my mother's nature to change her mind, so there was little chance of her backing down over the expulsion of von Tench from the convent guest house. I was still thinking about Bruno's suspicions of Captain Trevelyan as I walked a less than eager Gretel back down the Rue Carnot towards home.

The puppy seemed distracted, smelling every lamppost on the way, instead of just the occasional one. Then, after stopping and starting several times, she became suddenly excited and started barking loudly at a man with a woollen, claret and blue bobble hat on. As he approached us, any restraint was cast aside and she tugged on the lead, barking incessantly. The man had to jump sideways to avoid a sharp nip from Gretel, who was intent on causing him harm.

I dragged on the lead and thought the man would be incensed by the puppy's irrational behaviour, and tell me off for not controlling my dog. But, he did not speak, nor did he even look at us, but he simply hunched his shoulders and continued on his way as if the incident had never happened.

"Be quiet Gretel," I shouted at her. But the man was determined to avoid any fuss and seemed as self-conscious as I was of the people looking towards us from the other side of the road.

"Sorry, sorry," I called to the man as I jerked on the lead. But he just turned off down a side street that led from the Rue Carnot.

Gretel would have followed him, chased him even, but I held on to her lead until the man had disappeared completely.

When we arrived home, I told my mum about the strange incident as she made our sandwiches for lunch, but she just berated me for not keeping Gretel under control.

"She *was* under control, Mum. But she took a dislike to the stranger, that's all."

My mother didn't seem in the mood for a conversation on any subject this morning. I could not be sure whether it was Avram, von Tench or the Captain who she was upset about, so I decided to be on my best behaviour and try to take her mind off the whole matter.

"Do you want to eat lunch in the courtyard?" I asked, and wondered if she would be deterred from eating in the garden by what the Captain had told us that morning. I regretted asking the question as it was certain to remind her of the incident he described.

For my own part, I tried not to think about an execution in our new garden and Mum acted as if Trevelyan had never said it. I knew she had distanced herself from the remark to save me any upset, so I vowed to myself never to mention it again. I wondered if she hadn't heard my question, but she had.

"Yes, of course," she answered convincingly, if a little belatedly.

"Good," I said, in order to let her know that I wasn't alarmed by the history of our new home and I began laying the table to ensure that Mum had a seat in the sun and I had one in the shade.

Mum even tried to distract me from the courtyard story by asking about the incident with Gretel. Or, perhaps, she just thought she had been a little abrupt with me when I raised the subject earlier. I knew, you see, that we were both completely conscious of the fact that, if we were talking about something that happened in the Rue Carnot that morning, then we couldn't be thinking about the horrendous event that happened in this very courtyard twenty years ago.

"What was the man like?"

I had to think for a moment to work out who Mum was speaking about.

"He was quite tall and I think he had a West Ham United bobble hat on, although it could have been Aston Villa, I suppose, or Burnley. He had a t-shirt with details about a rock group tour on it. I can't remember the name of the group though."

"Did he have a beard?"

"No, I don't think so. Oh, he was carrying a holdall bag."

From suddenly being very interested, Mum soon dismissed the incident.

"Well, perhaps Gretel doesn't like bobble hats or holdall bags," mother suggested, and then told me a story about a dog she once knew that attacked anyone with an umbrella and it turned out that the dog had been beaten by someone with an umbrella when it was a little puppy.

"Dogs don't forget," mother added.

"I thought it was elephants that never forgot," I replied and she laughed, as much out of relief as anything else; relief that I wasn't shook rigid by the horrific story of events in this very courtyard. She obviously wanted to protect me from such matters and we deliberately avoided any discussion about the events of this morning.

I felt an urgent need to appeal on behalf of Ludwig von Tench, but felt my mum might think that I was taking sides with Captain Trevelyan, or that we were ganging up on her.

To be honest, I felt the same way about Mr Avram, although an appeal on his account could only follow a successful one on behalf of von Tench.

We ate our sandwiches in silence, each knowing what the other was thinking about, and yet hoping that they had not been unduly alarmed by the events. The great paradox for me was the conflicting positions of Kaleb Ben Avram and Bruno Fournier. Avram absolutely denied being responsible for the ransacking of the basement and Bruno was utterly certain that the Jewish man was guilty of it. If they had been on a jury together, it would never have reached a verdict and yet only one of them could be right.

15

Mum was right, dogs don't forget. The next morning Gretel led me off towards the sand dunes where we had walked the previous day. She either preferred this shorter excursion or she was following a trail. The latter alternative only occurred to me after I saw the stranger again.

The sun was up but hiding behind a slate grey blanket of clouds. I was wondering whether it might be too windy to return home via the beach road when Gretel decided we should take a more direct route back down the Rue Carnot. There hadn't been any rain for a few days and I had found that, in Berck, this often caused the sand to dry out and get blown across the promenade and down the side streets like a dust storm. At first, I thought it might be this minor sandstorm that was upsetting Gretel, but then I felt a sudden jerk on the dog's lead. I covered my eyes against the sand that was gusting around and looked down the almost empty street that led past the shops to our new home.

I was being pulled along the pavement by a small but determined puppy who was intent on following a man, who I quickly recognised as the person she had barked at previously. For my part, I was hoping to keep our distance, but then an opportunity arose. The man stopped and went into a shop that sold tobacco and newspapers. I tugged on the dog's lead and rushed past, down the Rue Carnot towards home. Gretel wanted to go into the shop and was just about to start barking again, so I hurried a little further along the street and pulled her into the baker's shop and slammed the door behind us.

"What's wrong?" Bruno asked as I dragged Gretel away from the glass door.

"Nothing, it's just that Gretel attacked a man yesterday and she has just seen him again. He's coming down the street."

I knelt down and held the dog's mouth in my hands to prevent her from barking.

"What man?" Bruno asked.

"Him!" I whispered as he passed the shop window, oblivious to the interest being shown in him from the three of us inside the shop.

"Who is he?" asked Bruno.

"I don't know, but Gretel has taken a dislike to him. Do you not know him then?"

"No, but he's carrying a case and a holdall bag, so he's probably on his way to the railway station."

The man looked different this time, as if he had changed in some way or was just someone who looked like the other man. It wasn't simply a change of clothes, it was something else, but I couldn't put my finger on it.

"He's changed," I declared. "Something about him is different."

I let go of Gretel's mouth and she pulled on the lead again.

"Gretel doesn't seem to think so, Peter. She's still barking."

"She must remember him from the kennels. How else would she know him? Because I don't know him," I admitted. "Anyway, I need to get home. I was just taking Gretel for a walk before breakfast."

"Here," he said, and gave me two croissants. "A little treat from me."

"Thanks," I replied. "They're still warm."

As I walked Gretel back towards home, I put the sighting of the man behind me and wondered how I might convince Mum that Ludwig should be allowed to stay on at the convent. I thought about telling her that the two men living upstairs were a couple, but thought this might count against him in some way. Mum was a tolerant individual who had no prejudices that I was aware of. She didn't speak about doing good deeds, as some people did, she just did them, without mentioning the why or the wherefore.

There was an old tramp who wandered the streets of Poplar when we lived there, and many people called him names and taunted him, but Mum always gave him some money whenever he passed by. And, unlike most people in our neighbourhood, Mum got on well with the immigrants who had moved into the streets around us over the years. There had always been some Chinese people in the east end, and then a few West Indian families arrived. More recently some Turkish and Greek people came from Cyprus and, if they lived near us, Mum always asked how they were and made sure they had settled in okay. I wouldn't say Mum was a patient person, but she was tolerant, which I think is probably more important.

There was reasonable doubt that Ludwig von Tench was the same Ludwig who had served at the Dachau concentration camp, and there was no evidence whatsoever that he was responsible for the callous execution of five French resistance fighters, but reasonable doubt was not enough. If I had learned anything from Perry Mason, it was that the best way to demonstrate that someone was innocent, was to prove that someone else was guilty. So, if von Tench was innocent, all I needed to do was find out who Saturn really was and expose him or her.

"Bruno gave me two croissants for us."

"Why did he do that?"

"I don't know. Perhaps he thought I needed cheering up."

"Why would he think that?" There was suspicion in the tone of her voice.

I didn't want her to think anything was wrong, and I didn't want to tell her about seeing the stranger again, in case it worried her. So, as we ate the croissants and drank our tea, I asked her to reconsider her decision about making von Tench leave our home. He has lived here a long time, I told her. If he leaves, then the Captain might leave too. She didn't speak, so I relented on my original intention and told her that I had seen the strange man again, the one that Gretel had barked at in the Rue Carnot the previous day.

"Did he say anything?"

"No," I replied. "I didn't speak to him. I just ducked into the baker's shop until he had gone passed. I think he was going to the station because he had a suitcase, or a holdall bag with him."

I looked at her expression, trying to work out what she was thinking. I hoped she wasn't worrying again.

"Bruno didn't know him," I added. "Anyway, he's gone."

"Good," she replied.

But I couldn't leave it at that. Something was bothering me, well two things actually, and I needed to get them straight in my mind.

"Why did you ask if the stranger had a beard, Mum?"

She didn't know, or she said she didn't know. One was the truth and the other was another version of the truth.

"I think the man who beat the dog with an umbrella had a beard," she said eventually. "They weren't sure, to begin with, whether it was the beard or the umbrella that set the dog off."

"Mum," I said, ignoring this absurd and poorly contrived anecdote, devised entirely to support a truly unsupportable lie. "I think that the man did have a beard when I saw him yesterday, but he didn't have it when I saw him today. Which is very strange, isn't it?"

I couldn't help noticing how my mother's breathing changed at that moment. In the silent pauses between my words, I could hear her drawing breath, the sound growing louder. It was a subtle change to begin with, her chest rising and falling in rhythm with the sound. And, all the time, her expression remained unchanged.

"And," I added slowly. "I think I know why Gretel was barking at him."

She placed her cup back on the saucer and looked directly at me. I could sense that, for some strange reason, she didn't want to hear my revelation, but she remained silent as if she was hoping I would say something other than what she expected me to; perhaps I would suggest that it was the bobble hat that drove the puppy to her anger.

"I think the man might have been the one who ransacked our house," I said.

It felt like the last act of a play; the curtain fell. Nobody spoke.

Suddenly, she smiled. "You have an incredible imagination young man."

I ignored her attempt to silence me.

"I think he had a beard when I first saw him and he then shaved it off."

The smile grew a little weaker. Why didn't she ask me why he shaved his beard off? She wriggled in her chair and thought about picking up the cups and saucers to wash them up.

"I am going to ask the agent about a telephone today," she declared in an obvious attempt to change the subject. She knew how much I wanted a telephone. But I ignored the comment.

"And I think he shaved it off because the police are looking for a bank robber with a ginger beard. I heard it on the radio the other day." My explanation was getting quicker, the words firing out towards her, like little darts, each one striking her, hurting her; but I couldn't stop. "If he is a robber, perhaps he tried to rob us too. And, I think Gretel recognised his scent when he passed us in the Rue

Carnot and that is why she barked at him. I think he is a burglar, a thief, a bank robber."

I had fallen into the trap that Perry Mason sets all his victims. I talked too much. In amongst all the information I had just passed on, was one tiny fragment that my mum could latch on to, in order to refute the whole thing.

"You heard it on the radio?" she replied, ignoring every other element in my long explanation of the facts.

The anger in her voice seemed disproportionate to the offence. I was still considering her words and trying to work out the cause of her disproportionate response, when she stormed out of the room and clomped her way up the stairs. I followed her, trying to get passed her on the way. I knew I had to stop her.

"It's nine o'clock, Mum. I have a lesson with Mr von Tench."

I didn't ask where she was going. There were only two possibilities. She stopped and pointed down the stairs.

"There will be no more lessons with Mr von Tench," she declared. "He will be leaving." The words were spoken with finality, with an incontrovertible certainty.

I reluctantly took two steps back down the stairs and she continued in the opposite direction. Captain Trevelyan had heard the noise on the stairs and he came out onto the landing, asking what was wrong.

"What is wrong?" mother asked in a quite obviously rhetorical tone, and she began berating the Captain for allowing me to listen to his radio during lessons. He, of course, denied responsibility for the offence. The argument raged for a few minutes as I crept back up the stairs as quietly as I could, in order to get close to my mother. I tugged at her apron until she stopped shouting at Trevelyan.

"What?"

"It wasn't the Captain's radio," I said, sounding as timid as Oliver Twist asking for some extra gruel.

At this same moment, von Tench came out onto his landing in the attic and asked what all the noise was. Silence prevailed for a few seconds and he called for me to come upstairs for my lesson.

"There will be no more lessons Mr von Tench," she said, sounding a little less convincing than she had when she said the same thing to me earlier. "I think you should think about finding alternative accommodation."

The advice was directed solely at von Tench and not the Captain, who received a muted apology before she returned downstairs, driving me ahead of her like a lost sheep. All the time, Gretel stood hunched, whimpering in the hallway wondering what was going on.

I sat in the courtyard reading for what seemed an age, until my mother came out to me with a cup of tea. I apologised to her, for worrying her so much and told her that I had heard the news of the bank robber on Veronique's radio.

"And you jumped to conclusions," she declared accusingly. "Peter, you have such a vivid imagination. You really must try not to think about such things all the time. Try to empty your mind of plots and schemes of murders and mayhem."

"Oh Mum," I sighed. "You know how my head is just so full of things."

She nodded. She knew she had asked the impossible.

"Do you see," I told her, whilst trying not to sound as if I was telling her anything. "Do you see, how easy it is to jump to the wrong conclusion? You thought it was the Captain who had allowed me to listen to a radio and it wasn't. Now you are in danger of accusing Ludwig of something far more serious." I waited for a moment before adding the actual plea for a stay of execution. "Please let him stay."

Mother had been impatient and yet I knew that she regretted her intolerance even more. She considered the consequences of her decision in her mind and pulled her seat closer to mine.

She agreed, of course, for she could never really deny me anything, which is why I tried so hard not to ask for anything from her, I suppose.

Later that day, she went up to see the two old men, in order to put the situation right. The day was set to end perfectly, when she returned downstairs and told me that the history lesson, which had been postponed today, would replace my maths study tomorrow morning. Ludwig had chosen an unkind way of repaying me for my efforts on his behalf.

It occurred to me as I lay in bed that night that, at least one person and probably many more, had attempted to find out the true identity of Saturn over the past twenty years. Perry Mason never took twenty years to solve a case; his best time for a master class of detection was nearer to twenty minutes. In the Case of the Frantic Flyer, someone suggested that murder is complicated and tricky. 'No', Perry replied, 'murder is usually very simple, it's the getting away with it that's complicated and tricky'.

16

Of course, it had not gone unnoticed by me that my mother's overreaction to a rather minor indiscretion had been grossly disproportionate to the offence. Mum didn't care enough about my education to warrant such an explosion of anger towards Captain Trevelyan. Education, for my mother, was all about work ethic, as she called it. The rewards I would get out of my education, would be just about equal to the effort I put in, there was little more to it than that.

So, why did she become so upset about my being allowed to listen to a radio during lessons? It was a mystery to me. Well, perhaps not a complete mystery because I was certain the cause of her rage was not this trivial misdemeanour. And, if this was not the cause, I should be able to determine what was behind her irritability. It could be the burglary and most people would assume that this was the case, but I know mother better than anyone and she was not a woman who was easily unnerved. 'Don't tell your father about this,' she would often say when something bad happened at home. Not that my father was there enough for me to tell him anything. Indeed, it was probably my mum's imposed independence that made her such a resilient individual. But, in spite of her inner strength, something was scaring my mother. In the Case of the Sinister Spirit Perry Mason was worried about his female client. Paul Drake told him that someone was scaring her. 'Well prove it, and do it quickly,' he was told. So, that's what I decided to do.

It wasn't the radio incident, nor was it finding out that she was wrong about the radio incident that created that fear. Nor was it the burglary, surprisingly. The obvious cause was the death of my father. It takes more than a few weeks to recover from the trauma of the sudden death of a loved one. Perry mentioned *delayed shock* when commenting on a murder once, so perhaps that had something to do with it. Maybe my dad's sudden, unaccountable death hadn't quite sunk in yet

For many people, ignorance has an incongruous sense of contentment about it, but it makes me feel uncomfortable. A little knowledge may be dangerous, as they say, but complete ignorance is like thrashing about in the dark. As a strategy for protecting me, I know that my mum would wish me to be kept in the dark about most things. And the fact that I *know* that, means I am not entirely ignorant. Contrary to her intentions – her very good intentions - I know this, and it actually makes me more inquisitive than I would be if I was given some information.

Mother failed to tell me, for example, why we moved to Berck. I know my father had died, but why should that cause us to relocate to a foreign land. I am determined to resolve that particular puzzle, but I haven't yet worked out my plan of action for doing so. There were more urgent mysteries to be solved, such as finding the identity of Saturn and determining why Gretel was so bad-tempered towards tall men with, or without beards?

Kaleb Ben Avram was certain that Saturn was Ludwig von Tench, a former Nazi officer who had served at the notorious concentration camp at Dachau. But, as I walked up the stairs to see that very man, I was not convinced.

It seemed to me that Ludwig von Tench had set himself against the world many years ago. Here was a man who was not afraid to take a chance, to move against the grain; a man who would take the narrow, more difficult path if he was convinced it had greater merit than the less demanding, more orthodox route. Whether or not he was that Nazi officer who had served at the Dachau concentration camp, when he arrived at Berck sur Mer, he turned against the regime and worked for the resistance. Everyone is agreed on that fact. Bruno and Veronique had said as much.

The people of Berck would not have permitted von Tench to continue living in such a small town after the war, had he not been accepted as one of their own. They could not have believed then, nor could they believe now, that von Tench was a double agent, the traitor Saturn. If Veronique knew who Saturn was, then von Tench could not have been Saturn; he could not have been that person, otherwise it would have been too easy and too straightforward for her to condemn him. In this respect, I was sure that he was the one person who could be ruled out. He was not, in my opinion, hiding in plain sight, as Fabrice Dubois had suggested, which made me wonder about the butcher's motive for making such a comment.

I think, it was because of my kindness to him, that Ludwig von Tench wanted me to know the truth, or part of the truth anyway. He was sincerely grateful for my help in enabling him to stay on at the convent. I think he would sooner have died than leave this place, in spite of all the terrible memories that loitered here.

Von Tench spoke as if he was connected to his home by some invisible fallopian tube, unable to leave, incapable of being parted from it. I had saved his life and I think he realised this, which is why he opened his heart to me that morning.

Some houses are happy homes and others are quite unhappy. Some appear sad just from the look of them and others challenge our view of happiness and sorrow. A lighthouse should be considered the loneliest of buildings, isolated on some cliff or island, the inhabitants living apart, estranged from society. And yet, it appears so enticing. People even buy small, colourful china or porcelain lighthouses to put on their sideboard or mantelpiece. A simple blue and white column, looking so bright, a monolith to the cheerful.

The convent had a contrary feel. A former monastery, which subsequently housed an order of nuns, a holy place, the holiest of places transformed from good to evil and now that memory of evil weeps from its very pores. Five men were brutally executed here, in this tiny myrtle-walled courtyard, once used for pious union with God. Someone I know made this happen; someone in this town is responsible for befriending evil in this holy place. I said all this to von Tench, perhaps not in the same words, but with the same emotion at least.

So, perhaps it was this eulogy that convinced him to confess his sins to me, as if I were a priest and not a twelve-year-old boy. It is easier, I suppose, to open one's impure heart to an innocent soul, as one might hope a priest to be.

He thanked me for the kindness, for the service I had performed for him. And then, without hesitation, he began telling me that one of the resistance fighters had discovered the truth of his past; he had found out that von Tench had, indeed, worked at Dachau or, more correctly, worked in connection with the Dachau concentration camp.

Leutnant von Tench actually worked in his home town of Munich, moving prisoners from the train station onto convoys of trucks, which then took them to the camp, twenty miles north of the city. It seemed an insignificant role to play but von Tench was not claiming his innocence, for he knew, or had good reason to suspect what happened to these poor unfortunates when they arrived at Dachau. His suspicions were confirmed when he accompanied the convoy there one day and saw, first hand, the horrific treatment they received. Seeing such horror changed his view of life and set him on another path.

"I applied for a transfer. I volunteered to go to the front."

And, as fortune would have it, this coincided with a change in Germany's military strategy. The army were bringing the older men back from the front to act as prison guards, whilst younger men, like von Tench, were selected for front line duty.

"Why did you volunteer?" I asked.

"I needed to do whatever I could to bring this regime down, Peter. However small my contribution might be, I could not stand by and simply watch."

"And Dachau caused this change."

"That and other things," he answered. "It was just one of many incidents that persuaded me. I was serving in Munich when the first allied bombs fell on that city. There was a full moon and the skyline was red with fire. The sound was indistinct at first, as the bombs began to fall on the other side of the city, then it grew louder, coming gradually nearer until, by instinct, we rushed from the buildings in case they collapsed about us. There were people everywhere, bodies too, some suffocated by the smoke or crushed by the rubble. The army records were kept in Sollin, a beautiful part of Munich, which suffered particularly heavy bombing that night. This is why Kaleb Ben Avram has such difficulty in finding my personnel records. Adolf Hitler was in Munich that night. I had visited that very bunker, if it can be referred to in such terms. It was a private, heavily defended room, beautifully decorated and furnished, which even had its own cinema. So, while the people of Munich tried to crawl from beneath the timbers and rubble, our great leader was watching a film."

I listened to Ludwig's confession, and told him that it was easy to see how Avram had reached his conclusion on my tutor's guilt.

"I suppose you see tiny pieces of evidence and thread them together," I commented. "Like the former occupants of this place, the nuns, threading the myrtle berries to make a rosary."

Von Tench looked at me a little strangely, wondering for a moment how I had learned of such intimate detail from the past life of my new home.

"And then, from twine, you have a piece of string, which becomes a length of rope, which can be used to hang someone," von Tench replied. "All things are possible in our minds; we all rush to reach conclusions about the guilt of other people, just as Avram does."

"I did as much myself," I told him as I walked over to the window. "When I saw the nails where the radio aerial wires were fixed to the window frame here, I too jumped to false conclusions."

"This convent was occupied by the Nazis in the war. I assume there were radios and wires everywhere."

He asked me to call him Ludwig, but refused to tell me the name of the resistance fighter who discovered the truth of his past. Well, he didn't refuse actually, he simply requested that I did not ask him to name the person. It was not important now, he insisted.

"I did have a radio but did not replace it when it stopped working last year." In truth, he confessed, he had become tired of the news coverage of the war trials. The trial of war criminals at Treblinka extermination camp were due to begin later this year, he told me, and these would bring to an end such trials, which had begun soon after the war ended. Ten officers, including the Treblinka camp commandant Kurt Franz, were to appear in October.

Ludwig had hoped that the continual reminder of those times might have ended many years ago, but it continued. The Dachau trials were held soon after the war and these ended in 1947, he told me. Concentration camp guards, medical personnel, SS members and even some German civilians were prosecuted in nearly five hundred trials which took almost four years to complete. He had never been contacted by the authorities. There was neither relief nor comfort in his voice.

"What if I am that same soldier who put those wretched people on to trucks at Munich station?" he asked. "I am not that same man now. If I was the same man now as I was twenty years ago, then I would have wasted my life. I am not the same man, nor was I even that man when the war ended."

I listened to him, his penitent head bowed, as I sat next to him, like a priest, listening to the reflections on his tormented life.

"What is the purpose of prison? To punish, to exclude from the world? To rehabilitate?"

He did not require an answer to any of these questions. He said he knew little of Dachau or what happened there and, when he did find out, he transferred to Berck. He didn't intend this statement to be an excuse for his part in the crime, just mitigation of his guilt.

"But doesn't Avram seek to prosecute you for the deaths of the resistance fighters? Does he not believe you are the spy, Saturn?"

"Yes, and with the same certainty that I am the officer his witnesses saw in 1940. What was I actually doing in 1940, putting people on a truck in Munich? What did I know of Dachau?"

He freely admitted to me that he was that man, but insisted he was not Saturn. Why would he open his heart to me on one accusation and lie about the other. He would do what my mother always did, say nothing. But, if von Tench is not the person who betrayed the resistance fighters, then who was it? Maybe it was Trevelyan, although how could it be? He did not arrive in Berck until shortly before D-day. No, the Captain was – like Captain Hurricane – working behind enemy lines and was wounded on the deep margin-sand of the French coast, along with many others in the days that followed.

"Do you think it strange that Veronique's daughter had a boyfriend who was a German soldier?" I asked. "I know he was only a low-ranking private, but is it not curious that she was seeing a member of the occupying force, whilst her eldest brother was an active member of the resistance?"

"Her boyfriend was a private, but not what you might call a low-ranking private. Dieter Weber was a Gefreiter."

I shook my head as the word meant nothing to me. Von Tench recognised my questioning look.

"A Gefreiter is the same rank as a private but the title is afforded only to someone who aspires to be an officer. Dieter Weber would have become an officer had the war continued for longer than another year."

Von Tench stood up and walked over to the small attic window and looked out, across the rooftops towards the railway station in the distance. If the wind was blowing in the right direction, you could occasionally hear the evocative sound of a train whistle blowing in the distance.

"I'm sorry the Captain told your mother about the execution of the resistance fighters in the courtyard garden." He hesitated, wondering how to best describe the background of such dark deeds. "Those were the bleakest of times, the Germans were expecting an invasion and thought the locals had knowledge of it. They desperately needed to find out and they killed five men in that process."

Once more, he paused before telling me that it was time we began the lesson.

"Just one last question," I pleaded and he turned around from the window to look at me. I spoke before he had the time to refuse. "Who do *you* think Saturn is?"

"As someone who has been accused of so many terrible things, I am naturally reluctant to respond."

"But," I replied, hoping and expecting to be answered.

"Bruno Fournier was and still is the obvious candidate," he replied. "He lost his older brother and his father's death drove his sister to the convent."

"But why?"

"You have asked your one last question," he replied and he sat down to begin the lesson.

After a French lesson, on Tuesdays and Thursdays, I would return downstairs and lunch would take a different course. I would repeat everything I had learned in order that my mum could also gain some knowledge of the new language. Unlike my maths lessons on Fridays, this twice-weekly lunch engagement was never cancelled or postponed. Mum definitely wanted to learn how to speak

French, she just wanted to learn it from me, not Ludwig. However, the expressions I learned were not always of any use to mother. I often made this point to Ludwig. Why would I want to learn how to say 'my brother' or 'my sister' because I didn't have any brothers or sisters and nor did my mother. But learning how to say 'mon frère' and 'ma sœur' would enable me to say other things later. It was a stepping stone, Ludwig would often tell me. So that's what I told mother.

"Voici ma grand-mère et mon grand-père," I said, trying to sound as French as I could and she repeated it, looking distinctly like it was a waste of time because her grandparents had died years ago.

I explained to her that it was 'mon' before masculine nouns, 'ma' before feminine ones and 'mes' with plurals, so my family is ma famille and my parents is mes parents.

"The same?" she asked, "the word parents is the same in French?"

"Yes," I replied and she smiled with relief, as if it was one less word she would have to learn.

"J'ai deux frères."

She repeated it, wondering how she could fit the opening into an alternative sentence.

"Jái deux grands-parents," received a similar response.

I could see from the expression on her face that she was finding today's lesson a little tedious, so I explained the difference between petite and minimes, just as Ludwig had explained it to me. Why were the friars who lived here called Fréres Minimes? I asked her, but she didn't see my point. Why were they not Petite Fréres – the little brothers?

"Because minimes means minimum, not little. So it is minor brothers, not little brothers. They were, presumably, a minor order."

"Even petite frère is a younger brother, not a little brother," I told her. "And frère also means friar as well as brother, so that's why friars are called brothers in English."

17

Curiosity may, or may not, have killed the cat, although I never quite understood why cats should be the epitome of curiosity. For what I saw of them, they didn't seem particularly interested in other people's affairs. To be honest, cats always seemed quite independent and indifferent to those around them. Nevertheless, curiosity may indeed get you into trouble, and it was certainly keeping me awake that Friday night. Conjecture and speculation wandered around my head, preventing any thought of sleep. Why would von Tench believe that Bruno was the informer codenamed Saturn?

I didn't tell Ludwig that the Captain had told me about his colleague's suspicions, although I assumed they had shared their views on the identity of Saturn many times over the years. If Bruno was the spy as von Tench suspected, then that would explain Veronique's claim that she knew the true identity of Saturn. After all, she was his mum and mums know everything about their sons. The Captain was less convoluted in his diagnosis; he thought that Veronique was the spy because that is the only way she could be certain who the spy was.

Every time I visited the bakers, I retrieved another tit-bit of information from Bruno. It is surprising how much detail can be obtained through conversation and a bit of idle gossip. His candour suggested to me that he could not possibly be the traitor for, if he were that person, he would not talk so freely about the events of that time.

Bruno told me that in 1943 the French resistance movement had 40,000 members, which seemed an extremely high number to me. I imagined all the people in Upton Park on a Saturday, all working to bring down the Nazi empire from behind its own lines. But then Bruno told me that by the end of the following year, this number had increased to 100,000. The hope of an allied victory was growing and this was generating support for the cause.

 There were resistance cells collecting intelligence and many more carrying out acts of sabotage, blowing up railway lines and weapons factories. As the allied invasion approached, the gathering of intelligence became vital. Bruno was the youngest member of the Berck resistance group, of which there were only about ten members. For whatever reason, that Saturday morning Bruno was even more forthcoming than normal.

Mum insisted that I didn't take the dog for a walk until after breakfast that morning, because she had an appointment and wanted to walk with me, at least part of the way. I think she was still nervous about the break-in and didn't want me to wander around the back streets alone. Mum needed to do some shopping for the weekend, but was also meeting the estate agent to see why there had been no more short-term lets since Mr Avram left. I told her it was because they had booked him in for two weeks and she had terminated this arrangement early. The answer was too clever by half.

"Perhaps you could ask them about the telephone," I suggested, remembering that she had promised to speak to them about it when she needed to distract my attention the other day.

"Yes, I will," she answered.

"I'll pick up the bread for you on the way back from the beach," I suggested, my offering an attempt to get back into her good books.

So, after Mum had stopped off at the estate agent's office, I took Gretel up to the beach. The sun had been out for a couple of hours, but it was still very cool on the shaded side of the promenade. We crossed the road and walked along the shoreline. I recognised the person sitting on the bench ahead of us and wondered whether he would say anything when we passed. He did, of course, but he was surprisingly very polite. Kaleb Ben Avram apologised for causing any friction in our house and I told him I was sorry that my mother had asked him to leave.

"I did appeal on your behalf, actually," I told him. He seemed to know it was the truth and smiled. I think his experience of life had taught him how to tell the difference between truth and the other versions of it. I told him this and he replied that truth has many pale sisters.

I was wondering what such an expression meant and would have left it there, but all the thinking I did last night had created so many questions in my head, along with numerous partial answers, all of which needed to be clarified and made complete. At the same time as I went to walk on, I was challenging my right to ask anything of this man, but I stopped and turned back towards him.

"They got it wrong about you didn't they?"

"What, that I am a Jewish Nazi war criminal hunter?"

"No," I smiled, realising he was making a joke. "About who you suspected of being Saturn."

"How old are you boy?"

"Twelve," I answered.

"Twelve," he repeated. "I was twelve in 1933, when Hitler introduced the Aryan paragraphs, the beginning of the ethnic cleansing in Germany." He then told me how his family, along with all the other Jews in his neighbourhood, were denied even the most basic of human rights. They were refused use of public transport and they were not even allowed to walk on the pavement.

"The black people in America complain that they are forced to give up their seat on a bus to a white person. The Jews were not allowed onto a bus, nor to walk on the pavement."

He told me that there was no heating in his house, and little food, which was only available if they worked; his family, as with all Jews, were used as slave labour, he added.

"We survived by eating the peelings of the vegetables left in people's dustbins. Thousands were murdered, the sick, the elderly, small children - anyone who was not productive. I survived only because I was a young man, able to work on building sites. When I grew too ill to work, I was sent to Dachau concentration camp. I weighed less than five stone when the Americans liberated the camp in 1945, twelve years and one month after the persecution of the Jews began in Germany. For most people, the war lasted just over five years. For us, it lasted over twelve years."

Twelve years and one month, I wanted to reply, because the preciseness of that remark had left an impression on me.

It didn't look like he was going to join my conversation about who he suspected of being Saturn. This man was trapped in the past; he thought he knew all he needed to know and my opinion counted for nothing in his mind. I was twelve years old, so why would he be interested in my view? How can I possibly hold a view on events that occurred many years before I was born? So I smiled and, once more, turned to walk away. He put his elbows on his knees and looked down at the floor.

"How did they get it wrong about me?" He was talking to the pavement, but I knew he meant the question for me. He was finally addressing my earlier point. I might only be a twelve-year-old boy, but I had something that he wanted to know.

"They got it wrong about who it was that you suspected of being the traitor. They all thought you believed that Ludwig von Tench was a double agent – that he was the informer, Saturn."

Avram wasn't as convinced as my mum was, that I was smart, but he was interested enough to find out.

"No, you are right about that," he replied. "I only ever thought he worked at Dachau."

"Even if he did, he is a different man now. The trouble with this world is that everyone thinks that the rest of the world thinks as they do, that they have the same priorities as they have. But it's quite apparent to me that they do not."

"You mean I am unchangeable, set in my ways. Some of those people you speak of might consider such a characteristic as a good thing, a quality, they might look at it as enduring or abiding."

He was much cleverer than me. I might win the occasional debate with my mum, but Avram argues for a living. I could tell this fact simply by the way he fixed his gaze upon me. That is how they teach boxing; don't be distracted by the punches, look at your opponent's eyes, not his fists, as these will tell you everything you need to know about what is going to happen next.

"You think Captain Trevelyan was the informant don't you," I said, with as much certainty in my voice as I could muster. It was a solid left jab.

"You are a smart young fellow."

He sounded like my dad. He was going to ask me how I knew, but he didn't have to. He obviously wanted to know how I read that in him. It would arm him for the future, for if a boy like me could see his true feelings, he was much weaker than he thought.

I told him it was his entries in the visitors' journal, the piece of poetry by Keats. Not that I really understood it, but the description reflected his thoughts, exposed his true beliefs.

"You wrote of the foot-marks of gray-haired Saturn, along the sodden ground of the margin-sand, almost dead, eyes closed and his head bowed, listening. It is just as I imagined Captain Trevelyan, when he parachuted on to the beach, in those fragile days before D-Day."

I remembered saying too much to my mother the other day and knew I didn't have to say any more than I had to Avram. If I knew his intimate thoughts, then the Captain knew them also.

"It's starting to rain," I said, meaning I had better head off home, but he just cast a derisory glance at the blue rim along the horizon and smiled.

"They call it *Jour J* in France," he said.

I tugged on Gretel's lead and walked along the promenade, sheltering from a shower of rain under the awnings that stretched from the shops towards the open sea, then ducked down a side road that led into the Rue Carnot. Without warning, the grey sky turned darker and a summer shower suddenly turned to a downpour, with rumbles of thunder in the distance.

My mother had already collected the bread when I arrived at the bakers. She had told Bruno to let me know this and to tell me not to be late for lunch.

"Mum went to the agent this morning to see if we are going to have any more short term guests."

"Is that what she told you?"

"I gave him a curious look."

"Your mother is a formidable woman when she is angry, Peter. And she was angry this morning."

Another curious look.

"She gave the agent a piece of her mind, as you say in England."

"Did she?"

"According to the reports I heard, she berated the agent for not telling her about the history of the convent."

"Oh," I replied, realising what he was referring to. "It was a shock to find out that our beautiful courtyard garden had been used by the Gestapo to execute members of the resistance. Mum was pretty upset about it."

He agreed but questioned how and when it was appropriate to tell us about such a horrific event in the history of the building.

"Buildings have memories," I answered.

"If that is so, it would probably be best for all concerned if it could forget them."

"I just met Avram on the promenade. He admitted to me that he thought Captain Trevelyan was the informer Saturn."

"I can understand why. I was convinced the Captain was captured and tortured by the Gestapo at the convent," Bruno told me. "I was taken there for questioning myself and I heard the sound of someone taking a beating."

His memory of those days leading up to the allied invasion was crystal clear, he told me. The events were carved on his heart.

"So much happened in that week. Trevelyan parachuted in, my brother was killed in the allied bombing of the airfield and I was questioned because they suspected I was a member of the resistance. I think they may have believed I was the weakest link, as I was the youngest member of the group."

Torrential rain clattered against the large window of the shop and the streets seemed to have emptied of shoppers.

Bruno's recollections of that week were indeed very clear, but I could not help thinking that they were a confused mixture of what he knew and what he had been told by others, for he could not have known everything he spoke of.

"It suited my parents to believe that Laurent was killed in an allied bombing raid."

Far better, he thought, to be the victim of an accident, rather than to consider what the truth might have been. Laurent was a leading member of the local resistance and nobody really knew whether he was, or was not, delivering bread to the aerodrome that evening. It would have been very unusual for him to be doing so, Bruno told me.

"But he went out in the van that afternoon and we did not see him again. We were told by the Germans that he had been killed in the air raid that damaged some of the landing and take-off strip and part of the building at the airfield."

He had to admit that it probably suited the Germans if the locals believed that Laurent had been killed by the allies. It added to the propaganda.

"The bombing raid provided cover for Captain Trevelyan to parachute in."

"Perhaps he was meeting Laurent," I suggested. "Your brother may have been his contact in the resistance."

I could see from the look on his face that this was a scenario he had considered himself.

"Did you not see your brother again?"

"No, I think his body was identified by Edith, I can't really remember. I was questioned a couple of days later."

It suddenly stopped raining and the bright sun that seemed static on the far horizon suddenly escaped capture from behind the clouds and threw a bright light into the shop.

"I better get off home," I said.

He nodded.

18

I was always a curious soul, well more curious than a cat, I think. I spent a lot of time at the library because I loved reading stories. My mum thought I was special, which is probably the way every mum thinks about her son, but this was a different kind of special. She thought I was clever, although Dad called me smart, which is probably not the same thing. I was top of the class at my junior school in English and maths, and close to the top in most other subjects, but I did not see myself as particularly clever; it was just that the other kids weren't that bright. In a world of morons, the half-wit is king.

There is a difference between wisdom and knowledge, just as there is a difference between clever and smart. Knowledge is about remembering facts, gathering information. The acquisition of knowledge comes from reading, so I am not knocking knowledge. But knowledge is not wisdom. Wisdom is more about judgement. Knowledge is what we use to explain the world and wisdom is what we need to understand it. Knowledge is seeing things and remembering them; wisdom is noticing the nuances around the things we are looking at, and understanding them.

It was probably on one of these occasions – those occasions when I blurted out stuff about knowledge and wisdom, that my mum became convinced of my superior intelligence. One day she gave me a note for my teacher, to let her know that I would be absent from school the next day. She didn't tell me what it was about, but the next morning, we took a bus to Aldgate and then changed on to another one that took us deep into the heart of London. It wasn't until we had to sign in as visitors at the reception desk that I found out we were visiting a TV studio.

Mum had submitted my name to take part in the TV programme Junior Criss Cross Quiz. We were told that most applicants were being processed in their studio at Manchester but they also organised regional heats around the country, including London.

Eventually, Mum was left in a corridor and I was led into a room with about twelve other boys and girls of my age. We were given a piece of paper and a man began asking questions. I was required to write down the answers. All the time, I had no idea what was happening to me because Mum had not shared her plan with me. The first five questions were rattled off, as if it was a competition to see who could write the fastest, rather than who knew the most. I had no idea what the capital of Iceland was, nor did I know the name of the Chancellor of the Exchequer. Why would I need to know the name of the Chancellor of the Exchequer? I was twelve years old and not eligible to vote for another nine years. I had a guess and, as I only knew the name of one politician, I wrote down Clement Atlee. Twenty minutes later it was all over and Mum and I were shuffled back out of the premises, me still bemused by the event and mother bewildered by the fact that Granada TV had found several children who were cleverer than I was. I didn't get to meet Bob Holness or Bill Grundy; I didn't even get to meet Barbara Kelly.

I told Mum about some of the questions, if only to find out whether I was correct about Clement Atlee being the Chancellor of the Exchequer.

"He's over eighty!" she told me, as if it was a ridiculous suggestion. Most politicians I had seen looked over eighty years old, so I didn't consider my answer was that ridiculous. It was probably the reason why JFK was so popular, as he was the only politician I knew who was under eighty. Of all the conspiracy theories around his assassination, I never heard anyone mention the campaign against youthful politicians.

When I next watched the programme, the winner received a pair of roller skates, so my disappointment vanished. The setback was harder for Mum to take however. It wasn't the prizes that drove my mum to it, because they were always pitiful. Roller skates had some use, but I received better presents in the bad times at home. The show even gave away dogs, budgies and fish as prizes some weeks. What would Mum have done it I had won a budgie or a fish? And she certainly wouldn't want a dog unless she picked it out herself.

The only compensating factor to my fall from grace was that nobody at school ever found out about my audition for Junior Criss Cross Quiz. The ridicule I received because of Martha Longhurst was sufficient on its own to damage my self esteem. I couldn't stand it if my superior intelligence had been called into question by the idiots at my school.

It was only last year that I had to fight Alan Dobey to protect my position at school, because simply outwitting him would not have counted for much. The idiot stood up in class and told the English teacher that I had cheated with my homework – because I had 'looked stuff up in the library.' The teacher told him that it was quite alright to research homework at the library, as long as you didn't copy the words straight out of a book.

"It's pretty clear from Longhurst's homework," she told dopey Dobey as she held up my homework book, "that Peter has not copied *this* from a book."

Her remark sounded a little too derogatory; I was hurt and I jumped up out of my seat.

"I told you Dobey," I shouted and I called him an idiot. He said 'shut up Martha' and once the class was finished we agreed to sort it out after school.   Word went round and the event attracted a large crowd. It looked like Madison Square Garden over by the sandpit in the park, except we didn't get that far. Pushing and shoving began before we even got to the school gates and then punches were thrown. He went down with my first punch but got up to his feet straight away.   And so it went on, I kept hitting him and he kept getting up. I didn't want to hit him so hard that he didn't get up and yet he wouldn't stay down.

"I'm fed up with this," I shouted. "Three knockdowns is a technical knockout." But the idiot had never seen a boxing match and didn't have a clue what I was talking about.

"Oh, look it up in the library," I shouted at him and walked away.

I'm not sure my mum ever told Dad about her attempt to make me a TV celebrity and the extraordinary episode was never spoken of again. It was just another example of mother's bizarre, self-motivated and unshared plans for me – like emigrating to France. If I had been consulted about the TV programme, I would certainly have objected, as I would have done about moving to France too. At the very least, I would have produced a list of pre-requisites for the move, such as protection of my rights to a roast dinner every Sunday.

For her part, Mum eventually made a valiant attempt to recreate a Sunday roast beef dinner with the foreign ingredients available. She never told me about the argument with the agent but I assumed the row must have been resolved because she had spoken with them about a telephone. There was a whole array of reasons for not having a telephone according to the agent who, in truth, could not be bothered to make the arrangements. According to him, not too many years ago there was a three-year waiting period for a telephone in France. And their most famous French President, Charles De Gaulle had once said that telephones were not necessary, and he did not think they would catch on.

Even when he finally agreed to organise the telephone, the agent made every excuse to deter mother. She wanted a new touch key telephone, but no, that was not possible. 'What happens if the keys get stuck?' the agent asked her. So she ordered a two-tone green telephone with a normal dial. I just hoped we didn't have to wait three years for it to be installed. Because the previous owners had not had a telephone, there was likely to be a delay, but Mum told him that we needed the telephone urgently in case there was an emergency.

"I would like to call granny occasionally," I told Mum.

"Yes, so would I," she answered, as if she was becoming tired of having me as her only source of conversation.

"Mum," I said, waiting until I had her attention. "What *did* Dad die of?"

A moment elapsed as she cast a glance around the room, as if she was looking for something that wasn't there. "He had a heart condition," she replied. "He had it a long time."

"But you said it was sudden."

"It was still sudden when it happened. It's still a shock, isn't it?"

I nodded and went off to the courtyard to find Gretel. She was lying in a shady corner and looked up as I arrived. She hesitated, waiting to see what I was going to do, and when I sat down she rested her head on the ground and closed her eyes again.

It made sense that Veronique's eldest son Laurent was not killed in the allied bombing raid. As a leading resistance fighter he was probably killed by the Gestapo. Perhaps he was, as I imagined, going to meet Captain Trevelyan, for he was captured on that same summer night and, shortly after this, Bruno was questioned by the Germans. I mouthed each of these assumptions silently and, with each one, Gretel looked up, wondering why she could not hear what I was saying.

Each of these silent statements appeared like pieces of a jigsaw – one of those jigsaws that von Tench crafted out of a thin sheet of wood, using that antiquated scroll saw that sat up on his landing in the attic. Laurent was killed, Trevelyan was captured, Bruno was questioned, and Veronique knew, or says she knew, who the traitor was. These all sounded perfectly credible assertions, but I still could not see the picture that this particular jigsaw was intended to produce.

The D-day landings followed shortly after these events, and any, or all of them, could have been an important element in the success of that mission. Operation Overlord was a turning point in the war. Any of the beaches around Calais, including Berck, could have been chosen for the allied landings. Indeed, being the closest port to the UK meant Calais and the other towns along that coast, were the most likely to be attacked.

When the landings were made two hundred miles away, in Normandy, troops had to secure positions on the beach and then make their way inland. Success for the battalion heading north towards the port of Calais would have been crucial, and support from the local resistance was central to a favourable outcome.

I was convinced that Captain Trevelyan was part of that plan. There had to be precursors to Operation Overlord. Is that why the Captain had given me a copy of Herodotus to read? Perhaps he parachuted in, made contact with the resistance and then acted as the trail finder for the allied troops. Someone would have been required to show them the way from the Normandy beaches up the coast towards the strategically critical port of Calais. There may have been

197

a decision not to directly invade Calais, but there certainly would have been a need to take that port as quickly as possible.

By the time I went to sleep that night, I had convinced myself of the scenario. Trevelyan was dropped at Berck, in that spot that I had found with Gretel the other day, where the woods meet the coast. He was hidden by the woods and the sand dunes and met up with his contact. That would have been Laurent, or was intended to be Laurent, but he had been taken by the Gestapo and questioned.

Is that why Veronique convinced herself that her eldest son had died in an allied bombing raid? It would have been too much to bear, that her boy had been tortured and had revealed something of the attack. How much would he have known anyway? He would not have known details of the mission beforehand, that would be too risky, too dangerous; the contact from the resistance would have received his instructions from the Captain when they met. Their mission, I surmised, was to find a path, a route for the allied troops to take from Bayeux, through Caen, and up through Berck to the port of Calais.

Yet, if Laurent was killed, what action did the Captain take to retrieve the mission? Trevelyan was shot himself and taken to the hospital at Berck, that much I knew. Surely, he would have been heavily guarded, so how could he retrieve the situation?

19

The following morning I climbed the stairs up to the first floor and knocked on the door. There was a call from inside and I entered. The Captain was sitting over in the corner reading a book, so I came in and looked around at the shelves, while he finished the chapter.

If buildings do have memories, then this room was the memory of the convent. Hundreds of thousands of words, all placed in a particular order by the Captain, as if he was the keeper of those words, filing them away in a secret order, that they may record every event that happened here. The quiet monastic life of its first inhabitants, the solace of the prayerful nuns, the arrival of the Gestapo and the execution of five brave men were all stored here. And yet, if this room was the building's memory, then the myrtle-walled garden was its conscience. The tiny courtyard had learned the piousness of silence from its first inhabitants. It had grown proficient in its appreciation of the art or skill of quiet meditation and it had learned the need for solemn contemplation at the sight of such an abhorrent act. The courtyard had been witness to both the best and the worst of mankind's achievements.

When I finally got Trevelyan's attention, I apologised to him for his being falsely accused by my mother. "And I'm glad my mother changed her mind about asking Mr von Tench to leave."

He smiled and told me that they would both have to leave the house sometime anyway. I wondered if he was being especially morbid, but that wasn't what he meant.

"Your mother says that your grandparents will eventually live here, when they retire."

"I don't think my granddad is retiring yet."

"No, perhaps not, but one day he will and...." He didn't finish the sentence.

"I could speak to my mum."

"Look, Peter, this isn't Black Beauty. Not every story has a happy ending."

I could tell he didn't want to discuss the matter. It was all a little too depressing to consider matters so far into the future, so I changed the subject.

"I saw Mr Avram up by the beach the other day. I told him that I knew he suspected you of being the one they called Saturn. I think I touched a nerve."

"You shouldn't always let people know what you are thinking Peter, especially people like Avram."

"My mum is an expert at doing that."

"Oh, I don't know," he replied, "I think she let us all know what she was thinking the other day."

"I did tell her that it wasn't your radio I had listened to."

Trevelyan heard what I said and, although he didn't acknowledge it, he was pleased to hear it. He selected a book from the shelves and sat down in front of me.

"I am going to work out who Saturn is; you do know that, don't you?" There was perfect conviction in my voice.

I was as certain of success as Perry Mason must have been about all of his cases.

He smiled again. "You will be the first to do so and it has been over twenty years now. Nobody else has solved the mystery."

"Did you know that Veronique's son, Laurent, was not killed in the allied bombing raid?"

The smile slipped from his face, but he didn't speak. Perhaps he even believed, in that moment, that I was going to solve the mystery, because I had taken a large step forward, into the unknown.

"Yes," I continued, "Laurent was killed by the Gestapo on the same night that you landed on the beach."

"So it was the beach was it, not the wood?" There was a hint of sarcasm in his voice and I had to accept that my questions on the matter had been terribly blunt.

"The wood is near the aerodrome, although it is not the ideal place to parachute into," I replied. "But, there is a spot, just between the woods and the sand dunes, that is perfect. It depends on how skilful you were at parachuting."

A half smile returned, but he still failed to speak.

"And Bruno was questioned by the Gestapo," I added, "as you were too presumably."

I wondered how much more I would need to add to my statement before he made a contribution to the conversation.

He was waiting for me to make my declaration, to announce the name of the traitor. I saw the changed expression on his face, as if he was waiting for me to speak a name.

"Oh," I said, "I don't know who it is yet. But I will work it out."

"I think you may, young Peter."

"Not young Peter, please Captain," I pleaded. "I have been young Peter for so long. It's the only consolation I have for the loss of my dad – to be spoken of only as Peter, not young Peter."

He nodded his agreement.

"The butcher Dubois is a candidate," I said. "After all, he was an outsider wasn't he?"

"I was an outsider, Ludwig von Tench was an outsider. There were other outsiders."

"But he wasn't a resistance fighter, either."

"And, he nearly went out of business when the Germans devalued the franc against the mark," the Captain added. "He moved to Berck just before the war. Not much is known about Fabrice."

It was a short list to support my theory and I wondered if Trevelyan was toying with me.

With the exception of Fabrice, I suggested to the Captain, everyone I had met seemed perfectly happy to talk about Saturn. Did that not indicate that they were innocent? Why would anyone talk so freely if they had been guilty of such treachery?

"Except for yourself and Ludwig, or course," I added. "After all, Mr von Tench was a spy by his own admission and you were clearly a special officer who had been trained to work behind enemy lines. And I can't be certain whether or not Fabrice feels comfortable, because he doesn't speak English, or not very well anyway." I paused, unsure of where I was going with the statement. "Bruno and Veronique also speak completely openly about the time of Saturn."

"I think it is time we did some schoolwork," Trevelyan said and opened the book on his lap. "As you are so interested in the work of Mr Avram, let us use the poem he refers to in the journal entry for some class work."

He then instructed me to write a short poem using the opening line of Keats' poem Hyperion. The Captain recited the first line to me and I wrote it in the exercise book.

It did not seem to me that Captain Trevelyan had been patronising in his discussion with me, although I cannot imagine that he took me seriously. I was, after all, just a twelve-year-old boy who, presumably, looked on the Saturn mystery as if it were one of his comic book stories, or a Perry Mason case. Whatever their perception of me was, I knew the reality; I did know it was a real situation that I was considering; I did know these were the lives of real people and not simply characters in a book or TV programme. My speculation and investigation was not intended to be some pastime, like completing an I-Spy book or ticking off sightings from the Observer Book of birds.

Almost an hour must have past in that hot, humid room, he reading a book and me scribbling notes and crossing them out again.

At the end of the lesson, he asked me to return the exercise book, so that he could read my attempt at poetry. I noticed that I had only written a few lines of verse in the exercise book and wondered if I might be scolded for my brevity.

He read it silently to begin with and then looked up from the page, before reading it aloud.

Deep in the shady sadness of a vale
where lonely bluebells turn their prying heads
towards the light and in that shadow search.
Where black headed gulls maraud the margin-land
that weds the coast in sharpened gravel thread
unto the chestnut, oak and silver birch

"This is really quite good Peter," he commented generously. "Your words paint a picture as expertly as any artisan painter might do. Was that your aim?"

"Yes, I suppose so. It's just a vision of the woods that run alongside the coast. The margin-land you spoke of when you told me what such a word meant in that context."

"Well, it's very good. Perhaps you should try to extend it."

"I prefer adventure stories to poetry," I replied.

"You should read it to your mother, then. I am sure she will be very pleased."

"She already holds me in too high esteem," I confessed.

He smiled and I wondered if he could remember his own mother and was perhaps, thinking of her at that moment, for his eyes seemed to be lost in past times.

That night, as I lay in bed unable to sleep, I trawled through what I knew and what I didn't know, separating the facts from the suspicions. There was much more of the latter, of course. A case could be made for each of the suspects and Perry Mason would have had no difficulty getting every one of them off the charge. Each person was both a litigant in the case and an advocate or antagonist of another party. Ludwig von Tench suspects Bruno, presumably because he feared for his life after his father and brother had been killed. Whereas, Bruno believes Trevelyan to be the traitor; and, for his part, Trevelyan reckons it is Veronique, if only because she says she knows the true identity of Saturn. Veronique makes a poor case out for Fabrice, based almost entirely on him being an outsider, but then, did others not fit that bill, like Ludwig and the Captain? And then there is Fabrice; I could not be certain who he believed was the guilty one, although comments seemed to suggest that he is convinced it is Ludwig von Tench.

Were any of these suspicions anything more than mere conjecture? I was not even sure that the traitor was one of these people; why could it not have been someone outside this group? I mean, who was the bearded man who Gretel barked at? And then there was Veronique's husband, her daughter Edith and her dead son Laurent. It could just as easily have been one of them. I accept it was difficult for any of them to remain impartial; too much blood had been spilled. And yet, perhaps, it was not very different from my dad's view of Charlton Heston. When he watched a movie, he didn't see Charlton Heston any more, he didn't see the real man, just the part he most remembered him playing. Dad saw El Cid; he just saw the character that had impressed him so much, he no longer saw the truth or the actor behind the role. So, maybe everyone just saw Saturn, the way Dad saw El Cid, completely blind to the person behind that disguise. If I was to discover the true identity of the spy named Saturn, I would need to understand the true person behind that facade.

20

The questions were still rattling around in my head the following morning. I had a lesson with von Tench at nine o'clock and, whilst he had been extremely forthcoming on my last session with him, I got the impression that he had very little else he was willing to share with me about the events of twenty years before. He was grateful for my intervention on his behalf but he had repaid me for that with his honesty on my last visit to the attic.

There was still so much I wanted to ask him about, but I was sure he either did not know the answers, or was not prepared to divulge them, at least not to me. Most of those questions could probably only be answered by Veronique, who had become the pivotal character in solving the case of the traitor Saturn. Like why she insisted on clinging to the falsehood that her son Laurent had been killed in an allied bombing raid, even when it must have become apparent to her that he was killed by the Germans? And just why did her daughter Edith choose a life of exile around the time that her brother and father died? Would she not want to be around her family at a time like that, not separated from humanity, cloistered away in a foreign land? I was beginning to see how lonely a life in exile might be, so I could appreciate the enormity of her decision to leave her homeland.

The other lingering question was how did Veronique's husband and eldest son meet their deaths? I wasn't even certain when they had each died. Laurent may have been kept alive for days, being questioned by the Gestapo; surely that was far more likely than the Nazis simply killing him for his part in the resistance. And then there was the question of whether Bruno was questioned before or after his brother Laurent was killed? Maybe Laurent was still alive when Bruno was questioned. Perhaps it wasn't Trevelyan that Bruno heard being tortured, but his own brother Laurent. Would Bruno not have recognised the voice he heard that day? Is it even possible to recognise a person's identity from a scream?

There were other unanswered questions too. It was only speculation that Trevelyan was captured at the time of his shooting. He may have been taken directly to hospital, because Veronique remembers seeing him there on the morning after he landed behind enemy lines. But, had he already made contact with the resistance? Was that contact Laurent, or even Bruno, or perhaps it was Veronique's husband?

I was leaning closer and closer to believing that Laurent was the informer. Laurent went missing at the time Trevelyan arrived, so perhaps he betrayed him to the Gestapo. The Captain did appear to be captured very easily and soon after he parachuted behind enemy lines. Who knows what happened after that?

As I climbed the stairs towards the attic, I resolved not to interrogate my French teacher, but to ask Ludwig just one question. That way I might get a complete answer. Better still, I thought, don't ask a question, make a statement and see what he says; that was how Perry Mason often retrieved important information from a witness.

"Salut Pierre. Ça va ?

"Ça va bien, merci. Et toi, ça va ?"

"Pas mal."

I stopped speaking French and began a more practical conversation.

"Bruno told me that his sister Edith identified Laurent's body," I said in a matter-of-fact tone, hoping not to arouse suspicion on his part. It felt as if I had jumped in with both feet and made a very loud splash.

He answered in a similarly disinterested voice, as if it wasn't a particularly important issue, but what I had just said could not be correct, he made that clear.

"There was a war on. Nobody would have been required to identify the body." He hardly looked up. "Anyway, everyone knew who he was. Only strangers needed to be identified and even that had no formal process attached to it."

"I am only repeating what Bruno said to me," I answered, hoping to provoke another contribution.

"Why would Bruno say that his sister identified the body?" I heard him ask himself quietly, a whisper under his breath and yet evidence that he was taking a real interest in such a tiny, seemingly unimportant point in the vast debate surrounding Saturn.

"He just said that he thought he remembered it was his sister who identified the body," I repeated.

Von Tench shook his head

"That cannot be right; it doesn't sound an accurate reflection of what would have happened."

"Then how did Edith come to see Laurent's body? Why would she need to see it, if there was no requirement for it to be identified?"

"Perhaps she just wanted to see her brother's body before it was buried. It is more likely that Edith's boyfriend, Dieter Weber managed to get her in to see the body before the undertaker arrived," Ludwig answered.

I thought about taking the discussion further, but he prevented this by telling me we would be learning to say the days of the week in today's French lesson and also how to tell the time in French.

Needless to say that mother was not impressed when I returned downstairs. She didn't need to know how to tell the time in French, she had a watch which overcame the need to know such trivialities.

I decided that I would take Gretel for a walk after lunch, rather than wait until the evening, in order that I could call in to see Veronique on the way to the beach. I told mother that it was to find out how she was feeling, after all she still had pains in her stomach the last time I saw her.

"That's very kind," mother said and I felt guilty that she mistook my selfishness for kindness.

She insisted that I must eat my sandwiches first and complete any homework that I might have outstanding from Captain Trevelyan's last lesson with me.

As we ate our sandwich in the quiet courtyard, neither of us took any notice of the sirens that sounded in the distance. Ambulances were often called to the promenade, to treat people who had exposed themselves to too much sun. The sound was subliminal; you don't hear sirens unless you are actually listening out for them and, back in London, they were far more commonplace than here, in rural Berck. Even the clatter of the police car alarm did not rouse any concern. We simply carried on eating our sandwich and chatting about when the new telephone would be installed.

"Granny will be pleased."

Mum smiled.

About ten minutes later, I set off towards the beach. I first realised that something might be wrong when I passed the bakers. The sign in the door said closed and, on the opposite side of the road, Fabrice Dubois stood outside his butcher's shop, gazing up the Rue Carnot as if he was expecting someone to arrive.

It was only when I turned into Rue de la Plage that I saw the police car and ambulance. And, as I approached the home of Veronique, I noticed the door was open and the activity outside in the street spilled into that house. Uniformed police officers stood in the street and the doors of the ambulance that was parked outside the house had been left open. Others, who may have been plain clothes officers, talked to the people who stood at their doors on the other side of the street. The engine of the ambulance was turned off, so it was not going anywhere soon and yet, there were no ambulance men around, so they were obviously in the house, treating Veronique presumably.

I wanted to ask someone what was going on. Perhaps I should have told someone that I was on my way to visit Veronique, but something told me not to get involved. It was a strange feeling because I could not remember ever worrying about getting involved in anything. In fact, I was always getting into trouble for stepping forward too often, instead of stepping back. So, I waited. The police officers would not want to speak to a young boy with a dog and, anyway, I couldn't speak very good French. I was just one of that small crowd which had gathered in the street outside, waiting to find out what was happening.

I stood as close as I could to two older women and listened to their conversation. Older women always knew what was going on. It was like standing next to a nun when crossing a busy road; nobody is going to run a nun over. Standing next to older women in a crowd is the same process.

"Elle est morte," said one.

"C'est tellement triste," the other replied.

I was not sure what the reply meant, other than the sentence began 'it is'. But I was pretty sure what the first woman had said. Elle est morte, meant she is dead. The facts sunk in very quickly, almost too quickly. They must be talking about Veronique but there was a lot of 'I' and 'me'.

You can tell a lot about a person from the language they use. The frequency of I and me in their speech, instead of us and we, or even he, she and them is an indication of a strong feeling of self importance, or so my teacher told me once. The change from I to them, is the process of movement from selfishness to the state of selflessness. Some people consider themselves a sun which the rest of humanity travels around and other people think of themselves as moons, travelling around someone else, someone more important than themselves.

This was a small town, a coastal town where there is no transient population. It should be no surprise therefore, that everybody knew everyone else's business in a town like this. It is not like London, with its Jewish community, Chinese people, Cypriots and others all jumbled up in a big mixing bowl, nobody knowing anything about anyone else, because they don't understand each other or, in many cases, they don't care about anyone else, particularly if they look a little different or speak a foreign language.

The other thing about rural coastal towns is that news spreads very quickly in a place like Berck. How did Bruno learn so quickly about my mother's argument with the estate agent; and how did he find out about that same agent not telling my mother about the executions? And Bruno wasn't the only one. On the morning my mother had the row with the agent, I saw people pointing at her as she went along the street; all huddled together in twos and threes they stood, just as they were now, discussing what had been said, or more precisely what they had heard had been said in the row between the estate agent and the woman who had just arrived from Britain with her son. There was an inference in the way that sentence was structured by the speaker. By failing to mention that my mother was a widow, it could easily imply that she was a woman of ill repute – she has a son, but where is the father?

Unlike Perry Mason, hearsay evidence had great value here in Berck; it was no different from the truth itself, just another version of it, in fact, just like omitting the fact that my mother was a widow.

So, the big question is, how come, after twenty long years, nobody knew the identity of Saturn in a small town like this? The answer to that question is simply because that name was only known to one living person. As Delia Street said, the answer is you'll never know, provided it is never shared by that one person. And now, it seemed, the truth was lost forever, for the keeper of that knowledge had just died.

The news of Veronique's death spread swiftly through the town. It began with 'as-tu entendu,' which is French for 'have you heard', and soon turned to 'n'est-ce pas choquant' which means 'isn't it shocking'. I heard both expressions as I rushed back down the Rue Carnot towards home. By the time I arrived, I was in no doubt about the truth that lay behind the scene I had just witnessed.

"Mum," I shouted from the hallway, "I think Madame Fournier, Veronique has died. There are police and an ambulance outside her house. I'm sure some people said she had died."

We met halfway on the stairs, Gretel scurrying around my feet, wondering why we had rushed back home and trying to understand what all the shouting was about.

Ludwig and the Captain had heard the noise and were coming down the stairs. They told us to wait in the house and they would go into town to find out what had happened. But mother insisted on going with them and it was I who was left, with Gretel, to wait in the courtyard, pondering on the events of the morning.

The particulars of what happened filtered through later that afternoon, although in reality there was no filter, it just arrived piecemeal, the truth and the speculation thinly disguised as the truth, all served up together. Veronique had died suddenly. The cause of death was still unknown. She discovered a burglar in her house. There was no burglar in the house. She died of natural causes. She was murdered. She had been ill for some time. She did not like visiting the doctor and, although she had been a nurse, she had an aversion to hospitals. The police are treating this as a suspicious death and believe she may have been poisoned.

As each element of the story was revealed, there was a pause, waiting for that fact to be denied or disproved. Some sources of information were identified as less reliable than others. The woman who spoke of the burglar was derided when she spoke of a poisoning. The day was filled with irresponsible assertions, contrived evidence and unreliable testimony until eventually facts began to emerge from the malicious gossip and the whispered hearsay evidence of the gossip mongers.

The police medical examiner believed that Veronique Fournier had been poisoned, so they were treating her death as suspicious. They wanted to interview anyone who had seen her in the last twenty four hours.

It was just beginning to get dark when there was a loud knock on the front door. A witness had told police that Susan Jackson had been to see the deceased woman on the previous afternoon.

"We are interviewing anyone who saw Madame Fournier in the two days leading up to her death." The

215

officer spoke very good English and mother invited him to step inside the hallway. He did so, leaving the front door open, letting a cool breeze drift into the house.

I wondered why my mother had visited Veronique without telling me. Why did she need to see her? What could the visit have been about? But before I had considered the questions, mother had answered.

"Yes, I did," mother replied as I hid in the darkening courtyard, listening to the conversation.

"Did you take any food to the house?"

"No."

The policeman wrote her answer in his notebook.

"Did you eat any food while you were in the house?"

"No."

"Did you see Madame Fournier eat anything while you were with her?"

"No."

Each time she answered a question, the policeman recorded it in his notebook. And with each answer my mother's reply got increasingly inaudible. She was asked to speak up.

She repeated everything she had said. She hadn't taken any food to the house; she didn't eat anything at the house whilst she was there; she didn't see Madame Fournier eat anything during her visit, she told them all of this information in a louder voice.

"Did you argue with Madame Fournier?"

Why did they ask that, I wondered. Had they been told of my mother's row with the agent? Had they heard about Mr Avram being expelled from our house? Had they concluded that my mother was a bit of a tyrant? Surely they didn't believe she was violent.

"Not really," my mother answered. The word *really* hovered in the still, cold night air that had invaded the hallway through the open door.

Why say *really*, when the answer was simply *no*. It sounded very much like Mr Avram's comment about having three children 'in total'.

"What was the purpose of your visit?" the officer asked unhesitatingly, not bothered at all as I was, at what she might have meant by *really*.

"I wanted to ask her not to let my son listen to the radio when he visited her."

The phraseology that mother used confused the officer a little. He tossed her answer around in his head to make sense of it. He spoke good English but the negative of asking someone not to let their son listen to a radio was difficult to grasp.

"You wanted Madame Fournier to stop your son listening to her radio?"

"Yes."

"And why was that Madame Jackson?"

"I thought it might make him homesick," she said and I recognised something in the tone of her voice. It was another version of the truth.

I desperately wanted to shout some advice. When it comes to the police, mother, there is no such thing as another version of the truth; there are only lies.

"We have only recently moved to Berck, you see and Peter visited her frequently. She was English and she listened to the BBC."

"But you didn't argue with her?"

"No."

"Had your son visited Madame Fournier in the last forty eight hours?"

"No."

"But you said he visited her frequently."

"Not every day. Not for a few days."

I sneaked back into my room as soon as my mother's interview showed signs of ending. But the police did not leave immediately. They clomped up the stairs to ask the Captain and Ludwig if they had seen Madame Fournier in the last few days.

"No," they both replied, although they had walked past the house the previous afternoon.

The following morning, news continued to filter through, and although the gossip and rumour diminished, it did not stop completely. The gossips had identified everyone who the police had spoken to, including my mum. The list was short, but quite surprising. Fabrice Dubois had delivered some meat there earlier that morning, on his way to opening his shop. It being food and her being poisoned made the butcher the prime suspect in many people's eyes. And, incredibly, Kaleb Ben Avram had visited her too. Him being a much maligned individual who lived and worked in the shadow of death, he came under close suspicion.

Veronique had said that she knew the true identity of Saturn. Perhaps she was killed because of that. She never hid her suspicions about Fabrice Dubois, which he denied, of course.

Initially, the police considered that Veronique was poisoned the day before, but they soon changed their mind, presumably on the advice of the medical examiner, and they extended that period to two weeks. Forensic evidence suggested that the poison had been administered slowly. If that was the case, then perhaps I needed to tell them about the strange man I had seen in town, because that was the time when he was around.

The following day the police returned to our house to question mother again. They asked her why she had not reported the burglary.

Who had told the police about the burglary? What had that to do with the death of Veronique?

As the police went to leave, I rushed into the hallway to tell them about the stranger I had seen in town.

"He has a very vivid imagination," my mother told them.

"Bruno Fournier saw him too," I declared.

The policeman asked me to describe the man and why I thought he was acting suspiciously. When I told him that Gretel had barked at him, the policeman lost interest.

That afternoon, I went round to the baker's shop to see Bruno, in order to find out if the police had been to see him about the stranger, but they hadn't.

"Is your sister Edith coming home from Italy?" I asked him.

"No, but she will be allowed home for the funeral though. But the police cannot say when that will be. They have sent blood and other samples off to the forensic laboratory in Amiens and say that the results will not be known for a few days."

In the meantime, Bruno commented, everyone is coming under suspicion, for he could not possibly imagine who would wish to murder his poor mother.   He was half right, I thought. It was strangers who were specifically coming under suspicion. Just as Fabrice Dubois was a suspicious stranger, an outsider during the war, and Kaleb Ben Avram is considered a suspicious outsider too, just as anyone from outside Berck could not trusted. And now both my mother and I were also considered as suspicious outsiders. So why were the police not making enquiries about the stranger I saw in town? Why did he have a beard one day and not when I saw him the next day? The police were not interested.

21

Perry Mason once had to handle the case of the vanishing victim, but never the case of a vanishing witness. I was left with a case and no star witness. The one person who knew the identity of Saturn was now dead. Just like Perry, I faced an unsolvable case.

My mind kept going back to what Kaleb Ben Avram said when he was leaving the convent. He was convinced that the person who burgled our home did not find what he or she was looking for, as no part of the basement had been left unsearched. The shelves, drawers and cupboards in every room had been emptied and the contents examined, before being strewn on the floor. If they didn't find what they were looking for, it was probably not there. What is it that someone thought we had in the house? Was this search connected to the Saturn case? There had been rumours about Veronique's house being burgled, but these were unsubstantiated and I didn't want to ask Bruno if there was any truth in them.

The town became a different place over the next two days. Everything came to a halt whilst we waited for the results of the forensic tests. Everything that is, except the speculation. That never stopped; everyone had a view on why and how Veronique had been murdered. Yet, all the speculation created was more questions, and even more speculation.

How exactly was the poison administered? Who would do such a thing? The answer to the second question was obvious to everyone. Veronique said she knew the identity of the traitor and it was she who had been killed. These two points must be connected. The killer must be Saturn. But why now? Why kill her after twenty years? What had changed to make her murder necessary?

I am not sure whether the local police were even aware of the twenty-year-old case of the traitor Saturn. So, they would not even question why any of the suspects in that case might wish to kill Veronique? Surely if they considered this case, they would conclude that the traitor is the one person with a motive for her murder. This person should be their prime suspect. Aren't the police meant to ask if we know whether anyone would want to murder Madame Fournier?

The fact that Avram had visited her just before she died added some clarification to my suspicions. Perhaps he had found evidence that Trevelyan was, as he suspected, the collaborator. Perhaps it was Ludwig von Tench who had killed her, after all, he said himself that one of the resistance members had found out he worked at Dachau. Maybe Avram found out that Veronique was the traitor and, unable to prove it, killed her himself. I was sure it would not have been the first time he had taken such action in the years he had been hunting Nazis and whilst Veronique was not a

Nazi, he might have considered her a Nazi sympathiser for concealing the identity of the traitor.

And, finally there was Fabrice Dubois, the butcher. Once Veronique had eliminated von Tench and the Captain, along with her own family members, there was only Dubois left. She must have confronted him with the allegation and he seized an opportunity to poison her with the meat he supplied her. All of these were possible scenarios, but none could be corroborated. What else was left?

I wondered if the police had considered suicide. Had Veronique poisoned herself and, if so, why? Was she the traitor and felt she could not live with herself any longer?

Even with all these questions racing in my mind, something else was troubling me too. Something quite miniscule, but it was nagging away in my mind. I went to retrieve the visitors' journal and looked for a particular entry. It was the observation about the garden.

'Pretty courtyard, perfect for relaxing, until we heard the history of the place.' Of course, it made sense now. The writer was referring to the execution in the courtyard garden. Five young men were executed in the courtyard garden, that is what Captain Trevelyan had said. It was a statement that shocked my mother. Trevelyan then asked her if she could really believe that the man responsible for such a horrific event could continue living here.

There must be a connection between this building and the murder of Veronique. All I needed to do in order to prove this scenario, was to eliminate the alternative suspicions from my mind.

And then, setting the murder of Veronique to one side, there was the other mystery; the one surrounding our relocation to France. All the whys and wherefores of this particular case had been pushed to one side whilst I considered the strange and sudden death of Madame Fournier. And yet, all the evidence was mounting up.

Like the drip, drip of a tap, the man with the ginger beard, the way Gretel attacked the stranger, the basement burglary, my father's unexpected death, the story of the London bank robbery on the news; it all added up to one outcome. The other version of the truth was just a big lie. My father had not died suddenly as mother had said. All the signs suggested that he was a criminal. He did not go to work in Spain, he went to prison. Why was it that our financial position changed so radically from one year to another? My father robbed banks for a living, that's why. He was caught and is now the accused at a trial in London. He had got away with the money and that is how mother paid 65,000 francs for our new house in Berck.

When I looked at all these facts together, it was quite simple. The stranger in town had ransacked our basement when he was searching for the ill-gotten gains of the bank robbery. Gretel recognised his scent and that is why she attacked him in town. The radio news said that one bank robber was on the loose and he had a beard. Of course, he would shave the beard off once this information was in the public domain.

Later that day, after lunch, mother went in to town for some shopping and I waited for Ludwig and the Captain to go out for their afternoon stroll. It was nearly one o'clock as the pair set off towards the beach and I waited until they had turned the corner before rushing upstairs to the first floor.

Captain Trevelyan never locked his door, after all, the front door was locked and only the other tenants had access. I sneaked about the place like a cat burglar, though I know not why, because there was nobody else in the building. I went to the radio and turned it on, leaving the volume down low. It crackled and fizzed a little and I turned the tuning knob slightly. The general synopsis was coming to an end and the newsreader was giving the weather forecast for Malin, Hebrides and Bailey. I had no idea where these places were in the world. All I did know was that the last one was to be subjected to southwest winds five to seven, increasing gale eight to storm ten. It sounded very much like a coded message to me.

The radio went quiet and I wondered for a moment if I had lost the signal. But no, there were those consoling and reassuring beeps and the BBC news followed. More race riots in the southern states of the USA; some news from Vietnam and then the latest from the Old Bailey where three men were on trial for the London bank robbery. He read the names, beginning with Peter James Longhurst. I didn't hear the names of the other accused men, or indeed how the trial was proceeding, I was just surprised to hear my own name on the radio.

I should have listened I suppose, but I was overwhelmed by hearing that name. The world raced around my head and I felt a little dizzy. My father was not dead and even though I had suspected as much and pondered this possibility many times in the last few days, it still seemed unreal, like an inescapable dream.

Suddenly, it occurred to me that I would need to tell my mother that I knew the truth. I couldn't keep this secret to myself. I could not continue these fallacious and concocted conversations about my father's death anymore. She would have to know. I would have to admit that I had listened to a radio. I would need to confess to the Captain that I had listened to his radio. I stood up and looked out of the small window, my mind was racing.

All I did hear, before I turned the radio off was that a fourth man was still on the run and there had been an uncorroborated sighting of him at Dover.

I was now certain that the bearded man had burgled our rooms and I was pleased that Avram was innocent of the burglary. However, it seemed a trivial concession in the overall context of things and now he was suspected of an even greater crime, because nobody had explained why he had visited Madame Fournier.

That evening I made my mind up to tell my mother that I knew the truth. I practiced it over and over in my mind and rehearsed the opening line so I did not get it wrong. Everything was prepared and my admission and revelation would flow from that opening line.

'One day,' I would begin, 'I overheard someone's transistor radio on the beach when walking Gretel.' Perfect start, I told myself. No need to confess to the Captain, no breach of rules; I heard it quite by accident. It sounded a perfectly valid statement, born of an innocent event.

'And the newsreader,' I would continue, 'said that a man with the same name as Dad was on trial for a big bank robbery in London.'

Okay, it wasn't the truth – it was, however, another version of the truth. The only drawback was that it provided one escape route. I imagined Mum's response, as if it was a chess move, delivered to negate my perfect opening – Mum's Indian defence. 'What a coincidence! The same name as your dad!'

Now, if that happened, I would have to own up, and confess everything. If she tried to bluff her way out of it, I would have no choice but to confront her with all the facts. It would be embarrassing but it had to be done.

Then, I sipped my glass of water and ran the words through my head one more time.

I looked up. Mother was sitting, sewing a button on a shirt cuff.

"One... one.." I stuttered so quietly that mother had not heard. And then she spoke.

"Granny and Granddad are coming over at the weekend and will stay for a few days."

She looked up from her sewing to check that I was listening. I wanted to speak but needed to wait until she had stopped telling me about their visit.

"Oh," she added, inattentive to my need to say something. "And the new telephone will be installed tomorrow, so we can call them tomorrow evening and make arrangements to see them here on Saturday."

Suddenly a host of other factors entered the equation that was being formulated in my head. Should I wait for my grandparents to arrive before I make this revelation. Could I maintain this masquerade for two more days? Perhaps they intended to tell me all about Dad and the trial when we were all together at the weekend. Maybe the trial was coming to an end and, now that they knew the outcome, they could divulge everything to me. If only I had listened to the end of the news.

I wanted to be brave, I needed to relieve the tension that was growing inside me. But I capitulated, I remained silent and confessed nothing. I just sat there wondering how on earth they would justify telling me my father had died. And, how on earth would they explain spending the stolen bank robbery money to buy a convent in France.

For the next two days, by hook or by crook, I managed to avoid any embarrassing discussion on the subject of my father's death. All the talk was of another death, of Veronique's passing from this world, so my task wasn't too difficult. I even managed to convince my mum that I was returning a book to the Captain's room when she caught me half way up the stairs, as I was sneaking up there to listen to the radio. By now I was desperate to hear the end of the news that I had missed previously. This close call was enough to deter me from any further attempts and eventually Saturday morning arrived and, with it, my grandparents.

After we had shown my grandparents around the house and introduced them to our two sitting tenants, I was given the honour of taking my grandmother for a walk up to the beachfront, with Gretel. I knew it was only a device created by them, in order that my mother and grandfather could catch up on matters of a confidential nature and decide, presumably how they were going to tell me the truth. And I complied, in the hope that I might be included in their secrets when we returned. However, the neat explanation for everything that had happened in the last two months came crashing down to earth when, for the sake of making conversation, I asked granny if she was coming to live with us when granddad retired.

"Yes," she confirmed. "That is the plan, but not yet. After all, granddad has bought the house as our retirement home for when he stops working."

What? Wait a minute! Granddad bought the house? A part of my neat jigsaw puzzle suddenly didn't fit in the space I had reserved for it. It was a corner piece to my picture of the great London bank robbery. The money used to purchase Le Couvent l'ordres des Frères Minimes was stolen from a bank in London, not saved up by my granddad over forty years of working for an insurance company. Had I got it all wrong?

Before I could question this revelation, another new and far greater disclosure appeared like a rabbit from granny's hat. It would seem that I had not been asked to take granny up to the beachfront in order to get me out of the way, but for the sole purpose of dear old granny explaining to me that my father had not, in fact, died, but had been arrested for a bank robbery in London. Relief, joy, fear and apprehension were thrown into a mixing bowl, made into a cake and fed to me as I sat on a bench at the beachfront with my grandmother.

"Your mother wanted to keep the truth from you until after the trial had ended, Peter," she began. "We are all very sorry for misleading you. It was a terrible thing to do, but we did it with your best interests at heart. Your father has been a criminal for most of his life; he has been to prison on two occasions, but has never seen the error of his ways. He loves you and he loves your mum. But he is not a good man and he is not good for you. So granddad and I decided to buy this house for you and your mum, so that you could start a new life; so that you could get away from your dad and to avoid all the publicity that would come with the trial."

So many people, it seems, abide in a margin land, living neither in the truth or in falsehood. My father did, apparently, or perhaps I was the only one who didn't know about his secret criminal life; well, me and the police presumably. Granny said he had always been a criminal, even before he met my mother. My grandparents were convinced of his unsuitability as a husband from the onset and had tried, in vain, to dissuade my mum from marrying him.

"We were disappointed at the time, Peter. But, sometimes, it is necessary for bad things to happen in order to produce good things."

She wrapped her arm around me like only a granny can.

"After all, we wouldn't have had you, would we?"

I listened to all she said. I smiled and there were certainly no recriminations on my part. I suppose they calculated that this would be the case if it was left to granny to tell me, rather than Mum. They knew that I would question my mum endlessly but, I had a different relationship with my grandmother and I could never question her.

The downside to a relationship like that, however, is that I would never worry her either, nor would I give her cause for concern. So I couldn't tell her about my suspicions regarding the burglary. I wasn't even sure if Mum intended to tell my grandparents about the burglary. Nevertheless, I was now entirely convinced that it was the bearded man who was responsible for ransacking our house. He must have been one of Dad's accomplices, the one who had escaped capture by the police. If he had searched the house and not found the money then, presumably, he had realised we did not have it. I remembered again about the advice Mr Avram had given my mother, that the intruder had not found what he was looking for.

As we walked back along the promenade, I was thinking about Avram when, all of a sudden, that very man appeared before me, sitting alone, looking out to sea.

"Excuse me a minute granny," I said, "but that gentleman over there stayed with us recently and I thought I should just say hello."

She looked at me for a moment, wondering why I was not going to introduce her. But she stood still, watching my every movement, without interfering. She wasn't far away from us, so I spoke quietly.

"I now know it wasn't you who ransacked our flat. Well, I can't be entirely certain, but I will tell my mother."

He thanked me and I began to walk away.

"We can never be entirely certain about anything Mr Avram," I added.

I hoped that this lonely man might recognise how easy it is to suspect the wrong person; to convince yourself of someone's guilt, just as Mum, Bruno and the others were convinced of Avram's guilt. Perhaps he could see this now and, hopefully, he could walk away. I wanted to say: 'you are no more guilty of that crime than von Tench or the Captain are of the ones you suspect them of.' But I didn't need to. He was an intelligent man; he could work this out for himself.

That evening the four of us played Monopoly and we talked about the future. Dad was only mentioned once, by me, deliberately in order to test the water, and whilst he was not persona non grata, I knew he would be mentioned less and less; he would die a long, lingering death, caused by his absence and our need to move on. At some point in the future, we would all live happily in this house. The *all* would not, of course, include Dad and it would not happen until granddad retired in a few years time. They looked at me, knowing how indelicate a young boy can be, expecting me to ask what would happen to the Captain and Ludwig, forcing granddad to mention the unmentionable, '*not until they are both dead*'. So, I surprised them, I kept silent on the matter. It would be an unspoken commitment to our future together. If granddad happened to retire before the inevitable happened, then there was always the guest room. It wouldn't give them their own living quarters, but it would suffice until the circumstances changed. We all knew this, we all saw the same future, but it did not need to be spoken of, no more than my father did anyway.

Because of the layout of the ground floor, it was not immediately obvious that my bedroom was directly above the kitchen. This is because you needed to go out of the kitchen, up the stairs, along the hallway towards the front door and then double back towards the rear of the house. I hadn't thought about it myself until I went to bed that night and realised that, if I remained especially quiet, I could hear everything that was said in the room below. Previously there had only ever been Mum sitting downstairs on her own, so this was the first time I heard the murmur of voices below.

Mum began by telling my grandparents everything about our new life in Berck so far. They didn't speak of the burglary, although I imagine my mum told granddad about it when I was out with granny earlier that day. It is the sort of thing she would share with him, but nobody else. Similarly, I heard nothing said about the Gestapo executing five resistance fighters in our beautiful courtyard garden back in 1944 but, again, this was something to be kept from granny. Tomorrow, I imagine Mum would probably tell me not to mention those two matters to her.

My grandparents were told all about the intrigue with Mr Avram and the spy called Saturn, and about my lessons with the two gentlemen living upstairs. They didn't yet know all the people my mum spoke of, but they did sound genuinely saddened by the news of Veronique's sudden death.

"She was poisoned," Mum told them. "The police are treating her death as suspicious. It is very distressing for her son Bruno, especially as he has nobody else to be with. He lost his father and brother in the war and his sister is a nun and she lives in Rome. He is a very nice man and gets on with Peter very well."

I was mentioned quite a lot that evening.

22

I woke up thinking about the last words spoken by my grandmother when she accompanied me up to bed the previous night.

"You're a thoughtful boy, Peter, but you must remember that some people just rush through life, clattering into situations, without giving them a lot of thought."

She was referring to Dad, but she could just as easily have been talking about her own daughter. The alternative version of the truth, so frequently used by my mother, was simply a mechanism for self-protection, often parcelled up to look like she was protecting someone else, like me. But she was not; these were simply a self-serving device to protect herself. I regretted having such thoughts, but they were not the product of loathing or annoyance, but more of sympathy as it meant she had nobody now that she could turn to and talk honestly to, and I wished that this could be me.

A couple of years ago, it was a different picture. I recall my mother regularly telling me the truth and instructing me not to tell my father, or not to tell granny. That all stopped. It became easier, I suppose, for her not to tell me at all, or to tell me a more acceptable version of the truth.

It is obvious now that Mum used this device to protect me from the truth about Dad. He was a locksmith working in Spain, fitting locks to bullrings for two years. There were some truthful words in that explanation but, together they formed an untruthful sentence. There were locks alright, and he was away from home for two years. But it wasn't Spain, it was Maidstone Prison, or so I discovered from my grandmother, who found it much more difficult to tell me a lie than my mother did. She knew that, one day, I would need to face the truth full on and, sometimes, people avoid doing that by inventing another version of the truth. I took consolation in the fact that my grandmother didn't think I needed such infantile protection.

Yet, in spite of my mother's frequent fabrication of the truth, I did not feel she needed forgiveness, because her purpose was always lined with good intention. The word *forgiveness* hung in my thoughts for a moment; there had already been too little of it and now I was making an excuse to avoid it myself.

If only people could forgive others as easily, or as quickly as they regret their own shortcomings. How many of the people in Berck believed they knew who Saturn was, convinced of that person's guilt. Everyone had a view on who the traitor might be. Actually, it was more than a view, some people were certain, just as Mum was certain that Avram had ransacked our new home.

If she could speak, I am sure Gretel would have an opinion too. She was convinced it was the stranger in the street who had burgled our house, and she was probably right. In all likelihood, he was an accomplice of my father.

It made me smile to think about the purpose of his search; as if my mum would stow away the ill-gotten gains of a bank robbery.

The following morning the four of us were sitting in the courtyard and we heard someone knocking on the front door. Mum went to answer it and returned to the garden with Bruno, looking a little less tense than he did on the last occasion I saw him.

Mum explained to my grandparents who Bruno was and introduced him. He handed mother a loaf of bread and mother's expression asked him why.

"I have closed the shop for the day, but brought this for you in case you needed it."

"Closed the shop?" mother asked.

"The police have been to see me with the results of the forensic tests. They have told me that my mother was not murdered."

"Thank heavens for that," said granny.

Mother offered Bruno a chair, so he sat down a little reluctantly and began telling us the full story, beginning in a very strange way, by telling us that his mother enjoyed eating small whole, raw fish. We all nodded politely, but each of us was wondering what the significance of such an obscure fact might be. Then I realised.

"Yes," I declared, "she told me. Her favourite dish was something called Ceviche."

"That is right," answered Bruno. "it is a dish of marinated fish."

Granddad still looked very confused by the conversation.

Bruno took a piece of paper from his pocket and read from it.

"My mother died of a disease called Intestinal Capillariasis," he said and we all assumed he had made a note of this when he was told.

"The doctors tell me that it is a disease which, if untreated is often fatal." My grandmother sighed and Bruno continued with his explanation. "The symptoms are abdominal pain, swelling of the stomach, which grumbles a lot. The parasites in the fish damage the cells of the intestinal wall, stopping it from absorbing nutrients. It is caused by eating uncooked fish."

"So your mother wasn't murdered," mother declared before correcting herself. "She wasn't poisoned."

"Well, she was poisoned, but not deliberately," Bruno corrected her. "If only she had gone to hospital it could have been diagnosed and treated."

"Madame Fournier had an aversion to hospitals," I told my grandparents. "Even though she worked as a nurse in one for many years."

Grandmother noticed my use of the French word 'Madame' and smiled at my effort.

"Thank you for letting us know," mother told Bruno. "In a way, it must be a great relief to you."

"Yes, I suppose so. It will enable me to make the arrangements for the funeral" He paused and shook hands with all of us. "I hope you will all attend. I will let you know the details."

"Will your sister come home from the convent in Rome?" mother asked.

"Home?" he answered, as if it wasn't his sister's home anymore. "Yes, I was allowed to speak to her the other day and will be calling her again when the arrangements have been made."

I was pleased for Bruno that he had avoided the painful experience of a police investigation, but I was saddened too. Veronique had died an unnecessary death, and the possibility of solving the case of the traitor Saturn had died with her. She was the only person who knew the identity of the collaborator, the man or woman who was responsible for the deaths of five resistance fighters and probably many others too.

Whenever I met the suspects in the days that followed, I looked at their faces, trying to see if there was any change in their demeanour. Was there one of them, who looked particularly relieved at Veronique's death; for they may not have killed her as had been suspected, but one of them had certainly been made to feel much more comfortable by her passing.

It had been a successful few days. I had solved the case of the mysterious Spanish trip, the case of the changing name, the case of the unexpected relocation and the case of the poisoned widow, although nobody was found guilty. And I had also solved the case of the disappearing dad, even if, in truth, that had not quite been resolved. That just left two open cases: the case of the traitor Saturn and the case of the missing roast dinner. Against all my expectations, my grandmother had played a central part in solving most of these mysteries and I was hopeful she would find a solution to the roast dinner.

I could not see how I was ever going to find out who Saturn was, so now the only matter to resolve was the future without Dad. Granddad had been full of good intention, I am sure, although buying a house in France was a little over indulgent on his part. Playing hide and seek with Dad was hardly necessary, considering he was held in custody throughout the trial and was now sentenced to ten years in prison.

23

On the day of the funeral my grandparents were undecided about attending. Granny didn't want to go because she hadn't brought a black dress with her. Granddad thought they should go, as there probably wouldn't be many people there, it being such a small town. In the end, he lost the discussion and they remained at home to look after Gretel. I thought that was a pity because the one person Veronique would have wanted to see on her last day on earth would have been Gretel. She loved my puppy and I'm sure she used to look forward to seeing her much more than most people.

Granddad was completely wrong in his estimation of the congregation at the small church of St. John the Baptist, in rue du Presbytere. It was crammed full with mourners, led by the two remaining members of the Fournier family, Edith and Bruno. Edith, or more correctly Sister Marie-Claire was dressed in a black habit with white headwear. You could not describe it as a hat, because it looked more like one of the kites that people fly down on the beach. She was much smaller than her brother in every way; shorter by several inches and slim. I might have described her as petite, but that probably has a different meaning in France. After the church service, the cortege drove on to the cemetery, which was situated outside the town on the road that led to Montreuil-sur-mer. I don't think mother had given much thought about how we were going to get from the church to the cemetery. Captain Trevelyan and Ludwig von Tench had thought about this though, and they soon secured us a lift in someone's car.

There appeared to be even more people at the cemetery than were at the church, but most stood back, or loitered a few feet away, allowing the immediate family and close friends to gather around the grave to listen to the priest's blessing. I had never been to a funeral before and watched procedings with interest, trying not to think too much about Veronique, especially when her body was being lowered into the cold earth. I wanted to ask someone how they made sure someone was really dead before they buried them, but I didn't think it was appropriate to ask at that particular moment. What if nobody had thought of it? I imagined them suspending the service and opening the casket to double check that the poor woman had been taken from us.

Not everyone came back to Bruno's house after the burial. A few people decided not to join the family, including the couple who gave us a lift; so they simply dropped us off and went home. But Bruno insisted that mother and I came in. I could tell he didn't want to be alone at that moment and many others must have thought likewise, because there was quite a crowd of people in his small garden when we finally went in. There were sandwiches and wine spread out on a table, and fortunately the weather was sunny and warm, as I don't think everyone would have fitted into his kitchen, which is where most people ended up.

Bruno introduced us to his sister as the new tenants of le Couvent l'ordres des Fréres Minimes. The expression on her pale face was changed by the very name of the place, as if a ghost had sent a shiver through her body. Edith was not drinking wine, nor did she eat very much. And she spoke even less, at least to begin with. She told us that she was allowed to stay for three days before returning to the convent in Rome.

"Just three days," she repeated, as if it was significant. She was thinking of another three days; three days in the distant past; three very important days in her young life at that time.

"You were a nun at the convent where I now live with my mother," I told her, rather than ask her, but I was wrong apparently.

"No, the sisters had moved from that building just before I became a novice. They were expelled by the Gestapo who took the building over and used it as their headquarters just before the allied invasion of France. That was about two or three weeks before I left with them to go to Rome, so I never stayed at the convent. In the interim, the sisters were housed by any families who had a bedroom available in Berck, whilst the sisters awaited their transfer to Italy."

Edith was reluctant to speak of her vocation, or what she did each day. I assumed it was praying, rather than good works, although I didn't really know.

A couple of hours later, when people began leaving the gathering, mother told Bruno that we had to leave too, as her parents were staying with us for another couple of days. He said that he would pop round to say goodbye to them before they left. To be polite, I asked Edith what she was doing during the remainder of her short stay and, in poorer English than her brother spoke, she told me she had nothing planned.

"I walk my dog twice a day along the beach. Would you like to walk with us? You could tell me something about the town you were brought up in."

She said she would like that very much and we agreed to meet at nine o'clock the following morning.

Gretel got a bit excited when she realised that we were being accompanied on our morning walk. She needed to snuffle around our new friend in order that she got to know her scent. When Gretel eventually calmed down, we set off along the Rue Carnot towards the beach and I asked Edith if she had ever watched Perry Mason. She said that the nuns were not allowed to watch TV, which made me want to ask how she knew who Perry Mason was then. But I thought it would sound like a trick question, as if I was cross-examining her. She might not watch TV, I concluded, but she was not entirely detached from human life. Surely everyone knew who Perry Mason was.

Edith was not wearing her full nun's habit, but chose to wear a close fitting white cap and a black veil that draped behind her. Even though I could only see her face, she was very beautiful. My grandmother would have been shocked by her beauty because I am sure she would have seen it as a waste. I remember when a young man we knew became a priest and she declared loudly: "But he's such a handsome lad." Everyone knew what she meant.

"There was an episode last year called the Case of the Notorious Nun," I told Edith. "Perry Mason had to defend a nun who was accused of killing a priest. The priest was being investigated for misusing church funds." I went to add to my outline of the story when I suddenly remembered that the nun was accused of having an affair with the priest. I withheld this piece of delicate information. "The nun was played by an actress called Michele Greene. She looked quite a bit like you actually; perhaps that was why she was chosen to play the part of a nun."

"Did she get off?"

"Oh, Perry Mason never loses a case," I said, wondering how I might correct her incorrect phraseology, without sounding too patronising. "It's wrong to say someone got off, or that's what my mum says, because the nun was innocent. Guilty people should never get away with anything," I told her. "I'm sure Perry Mason wouldn't be a party to that."

"What about your dad?" she asked, noticing that I never mentioned him.

I told her the full story, or at least everything I had been told or worked out for myself.

"Do you miss him?"

"Of course, but it gets better every day. What about your dad, do you miss him?"

"Of course," she repeated back to me, "but, for me, it gets worse every day."

I regretted touching a nerve, raking up the past, because it was clearly still painful. Sometimes, the truth needs help to wake it from its drowsiness and separate it from the other versions that would diminish its worth. This seemed like one of those times.

"People tell me," I said, trying not to sound too conceited, "that I am a good listener for my age. Your mum said so actually."

It went quiet and I sensed that she wanted to tell me something. It felt like she had always wanted to tell someone something, but had been prevented from doing so. Now, only her brother was left and often we don't tell our innermost thoughts to those closest to us, for fear that we might cause them pain too. Pain, like a problem is rarely shared or halved as people say, but more often, it is doubled by sharing it with someone who really cares about you.

Sister Marie Claire, Edith could tell a priest, I suppose. Perhaps she had done so, but confessing something to God, emptying your soul to a priest is not, I imagine, the same as emptying your heart to a friend. I was almost a stranger and she met few people outside the convent. Maybe that is why she chose me, but I was pleased that she did.

I was explaining to her that, whilst my mother and I had only lived in Berck for a short period, I had got to know Edith's mother quite well and visited her on most days. But, suddenly, Edith interrupted me. It was out of character for her, because she was herself a good listener, making sure that you had finished speaking before replying. But she was overpowered by an urge to speak and she could resist it no longer.

"Do you know about the events that caused me to leave this town?" she asked.

"Yes, I do," I answered, remembering that good listeners say as little as possible.

"It was all my fault."

I waited but that was all she said. The statement sounded incomplete, but then it felt as if she was not going to say anything else on the matter; that all she needed to do, in order to empty her soul, was to say those five words. Seconds went by, then minutes it seemed, and the only sounds I heard was her whispering the Latin words 'mea culpe'. The words were breathed, rather than spoken and cast to the wind to be taken heavenward, like the pious smoke from an incense burner. Even Gretel looked up at us strangely, wondering why we had stopped talking. Something had to be said.

"Are you... were you the traitor? Were you Saturn?" I asked hesitantly.

She stopped walking and looked directly at me, suddenly realising that I knew much more than she had thought. She walked to a bench and sat down. I sat next to her and for a moment we just looked out across the wide sandy beach towards a hardly visible sea in the distance.

"I had a boyfriend," she stuttered.

"Gefreiter Dieter Weber," I replied and regretted it immediately, as it made me sound a little too knowing and I thought it might cause her to remain silent on such important issues. But I'm not sure she was paying very much attention to what I said anyway. She seemed to be gazing, dreamily into the past, or perhaps praying to an unseen God.

"He was just a boy and I was just a girl. He had a position of trust with the Gestapo."

"I'm not sure the Gestapo deserve anybody's trust."

I reprimanded myself silently for interrupting her and cautioned myself inwardly to simply listen to her story. Stop trying to be clever.

She paused between sentences, to consider what she was going to say. At first I thought it was because she lived in a silent order and was not used to speaking. But then, you never forget how to speak do you? She probably hadn't spoken much English for some time, because the accent she had picked up from her mother, gradually returned.

"When my brother Laurent was killed, I told Dieter that I wanted to see him; I wanted to see Laurent one more time; to touch him, to see with my own eyes that he was dead. Otherwise, I thought I might never be able to accept that he was dead. Dieter took me, of course; he would do anything for me. We had been told that Laurent was killed in an allied bombing raid at the aerodrome, so I was expecting to be shocked by his wounds."

She hesitated and began to cry. I offered her my hankie but she simply wiped the tears away and continued with her story.

"Dieter had not seen the body. It was completely covered with a white sheet. The lights were out in the building and we sneaked in. Dieter had a torch, which I took from him and he pulled the sheet away from Laurent. It was the cuts and bruises on his face that I saw first. I shone the torch at his bruised face, then at his arms and legs. The wounds were not at all like I was expecting and it was clear that his injuries had not been caused by a bomb. Laurent had been tied up, you could see where the straps or rope had cut into his wrists. There were more bruises to his body, and his fingers had been broken, they were misshapen and pointing in different directions. Three of the fingers on his left hand were still purple with bruising and the finger nails were missing."

She paused again and this time took the handkerchief from me. Gretel looked at her, wondering what was going on.

"Dieter was horrified; he didn't realise what we were going to see. He wasn't aware that Laurent had been tortured. He was just showing me the body as I had asked him to do. I truly believe he thought that Laurent had been killed in the allied bombing raid, as we had all been told. He quickly covered the body up with the sheet and dragged me sobbing from the building, telling me all the time to be quiet in case someone heard us."

Everything changed that day, she told me. The world became a different place. She repeated the statement about her boyfriend and, at first, I wondered if she was trying to convince herself that Dieter did not know that her brother had been tortured. But it was clear that he did not, otherwise he would not have shown her the body.

"Dieter was as shocked as I was when we saw Laurent's body. He pleaded with me not to tell my father what I had seen. He assured me that no harm could come to me. I thought he meant that he would look after me, that Dieter would ensure that nothing bad would happen to me. Yet, this was not what he had said. He did not say 'no harm would come to me', he said 'no harm could come to me', which seemed to me, to mean something entirely different. It was a moment or two before I realised what he meant. I suddenly understood the significance of those words and I am sure he saw that recognition in my eyes. He meant that no harm could come to me because that was the deal, but I knew that the deal was nothing to do with him. In that second, I knew the truth. An agreement had been made between my father and the Gestapo. No harm would come to his family provided he co-operated with them. That is why Dieter made the point of saying that I should not tell my father what I had seen."

Edith stood up and paced up and down, looking at the floor. Some fears must have rested in her mind about her father, some subliminal thing that she had seen must have prompted her suspicions.

"I don't know why I am telling you all this, Peter. I'm sorry, it is very unfair, you are just a child."

"I think I'm aware of much more than you believe Edith."

"I have not been called Edith for so long."

"Would you prefer I call you Sister Marie-Claire?"

She smiled and I wondered why it was such a rare event, for it was a lovely smile, generous, if a little bit melancholy and beauty is always enhanced with a smile.

I wondered if that smile meant that she was ready for me to tell her everything I had learned in my short stay here in Berck. So, I told her what I knew, about the executions in the courtyard garden, about Ludwig von Tench acting as a spy for the resistance, the suspicions everyone had about the outsider Fabrice Dubois, the fact that I already knew that the Germans had lied to her family about how Laurent had died and finally I told her about Captain Trevelyan's mission in the days just before D-day. I even told her where I think he landed, between the sand dunes and the wood.

"But that bit is speculation," I told her. "And I don't know what happened after D-day, or *Jour J* as you call it in France," I added, wondering if I had said too much.

I thought I heard a sigh of relief that she did not have to explain all that detail to me.

"I had even guessed that your brother Laurent had been tortured by the Gestapo."

"What don't you know then?"

"I don't know who Saturn is."

I expected her to say that nobody knows that, well, not now her mother had died, but she didn't. I was surprised by that.

"I didn't tell anyone what I had seen," she said, "at least not at that time. I feared that if I said anything there would be reprisals; Dieter could be punished for allowing me to see the body, my parents and Bruno would want revenge. I wasn't even sure about my father being the traitor, because Dieter had not actually said the words, it was just the look on his face when he said that nothing could happen to me. So, I kept silent. You have to understand that my parents believed that Laurent had been killed by an allied bomb and, if enough people believe something to be true, in time it becomes the truth."

"Or another version of the truth," I suggested.

She looked at me a little strangely.

"It's just something my mother says," I told her.

She explained that, two days later, Bruno was picked up for questioning by the Gestapo. Edith could not be sure what her brother Laurent had disclosed under torture. He may have named members of the resistance, including Bruno and her father. Later that same day she met Dieter; he was worried that she may have said something about the discovery they had made together. He pleaded with her to remain silent.

"Dieter told me that these were dangerous times." Her voice trembled at the recollection of his words. "It is not easy to forget such prophetic comments." She paused for a moment to collect her thoughts. "He gave me a gun."

"A gun?"

"A pistol. Most of the soldiers had taken guns from their dead enemies on a battlefield and kept them. It was loaded and he wanted me to keep it for protection, in case anybody came for me. It was as if he knew something was going to happen. He knew that something had changed with the torture of Laurent."

All this came about, she told me, in those final days before the allied invasion, although the actual sequence of events was difficult to remember after so many years had elapsed. She could recall the exact details of conversations she had with Dieter and others, but the order of events had become confused in her mind.

"I told Dieter that I would keep my silence, as long as he was honest with me and told me everything he knew."

Edith remembered that, whilst Bruno was still being questioned by the Gestapo, her father had taken himself off to demand his release. That is what her father told Edith and her mother when he returned home.

"It was that same day, I think, that mother discovered the pistol in my room."

It caused an argument, she said, and her mother told her that she must stop seeing Dieter.

"I should leave the work of the resistance to the men, my mother told me angrily."

And yet it was strange that Veronique did not take the gun from her daughter. She knew, as well as anyone, I suppose, that the situation was worsening. The Gestapo had set up their headquarters at the convent and more German troops were being moved into the coastal towns around Calais. That evening, the Gestapo released Bruno. He was unharmed and this only reinforced the suspicions that Edith had about her father.

"If I was right and no harm could come to me, then none could come to Bruno either."

At dawn of the following day five young men, all members of the resistance, were seized from their beds, arrested and executed in the courtyard at the convent. It was impossible to establish what had caused this event, she told me. Bruno insisted that he had been interrogated but not tortured and he had disclosed nothing to them. All day, rumours circulated about who had betrayed them, but the speculation had no foundation. The Germans were becoming increasingly suspicious, more agitated and progressively more violent towards the citizens of Berck.

That evening there were new rumours, whispers of an invasion at Calais and the defences on the beaches along the coastline, including Berck itself were reinforced by the Germans.

"I did not sleep that night, wondering what had led to the arrest and execution of our young men," she said. "Had it been Laurent who disclosed their identity, or had it been Bruno? I wasn't aware that my father had been interviewed too. I thought he had just gone to the Gestapo to plead for Bruno's release."

It was not until Edith saw Dieter the following day that everything became clear to her and even then, she could not tell anyone what she had been told, or Dieter would have been executed as a traitor.

"He told me," she said, her voice quivering as she spoke. "He told me that the Gestapo had turned my father, they had convinced him that the allies had killed his eldest son in the bombing raid. They told him that Bruno would die soon too, if he continued to follow his brother's footsteps. The resistance would be responsible for the deaths of both his sons. The propaganda of an allied victory was nonsense, the Gestapo officers told him; life would be much simpler if the locals accepted life under the German authorities. He could continue his bakery business, which Bruno would inherit after him. Life could return to normal. That is what they told my father."

Edith knew all this, she told me, because Dieter Weber had told her everything he knew.

"You must understand," she added, "that the war had become part of our life; it had been our life for the last five years. What the authorities had told my father made sense. In his mind, it made perfect sense."

Dieter also told Edith that the allied bombing of the airfield had been ineffective and more aircraft had arrived there over the last few days. Laurent had let the allies know that the airfield was still fully operational; it was probably his last act in this terrible war. He was caught by the Gestapo whilst carrying out reconnaissance at the airfield. They tortured and killed him and then blamed the allied bombing for his death. It was von Tench who had warned Laurent about the reinforcements at the airfield and he took great risk doing so.

Whether it was British propaganda or simply fraying nerves on the part of the Germans, but the rumours of an allied invasion along the Calais coast, and even in Berck itself, increased further that day. Edith stopped speaking, as if she was trying again to remember the sequence of events. Which day was she now talking about?

"It was Sunday," she said in a moment of sudden realisation. "Of course, it was Sunday and the church bells were ringing."

I looked out towards the distant horizon. The sun was high in the sky and more people were taking to the beach. Some were swimming in the sea and others flying kites or eating ice creams. It was difficult to relate the story she was telling me to the unwarlike scene that we saw before us. She did, eventually continue.

Edith told me that her father was Saturn, he was the traitor. He gave information to the Nazis in exchange for the protection of his family. This is why the Germans could not allow him to find out that Laurent had been tortured. That is why they told him that his son had been killed in an allied bombing raid. Edith confronted her father but he denied it. The very next day she was told that Dieter was dead.

"He had been killed by the resistance, the Germans told me but, of course, I knew this to be a lie."

"But they must have known that," I answered. "They must have realised that you would have known that was a lie."

"Of course they did," she replied. "But, by then, on that overcast Monday morning, the war had changed. The need for Saturn had passed."

She had learned all the facts after the war; why wouldn't she, because that day changed her life. The allies required a full moon and a low tide and these were only available on the Monday, Tuesday and Wednesday of that week. The plan was to attack on the Monday, but the light cloud cover and winds they needed was not forecast. A low-pressure trough came across the North Atlantic and drifted into the English Channel. The weather prevented the invasion that Monday and, in a way, she told me, it worked in the allies favour, because it rather proved all the rumours were wrong. Everyone said there would be an invasion along the Calais coast that Monday and it didn't happen. But the great sigh of relief from the Germans in Berck was proved to be misplaced because the next day, news arrived of the landings in Normandy.

24

Knowing that the allied invasion was planned for the Monday, Captain Trevelyan parachuted on to the beach the previous Friday night, landing between the dunes and the wood, just where I had imagined him doing so.

Under the shadow of a waxing moon, the Captain expected to meet Laurent Fournier but, instead, he found himself surrounded by German troops intent on taking him alive. He charged the troops like a one-man army, determined to take as many enemy lives as he could. He was brought down by a bullet to his right shoulder, which meant he couldn't hold the gun. He was overpowered and would have been questioned there and then, on the beach, except the Gestapo feared he might die and they would not recover from him the vital information they needed about the invasion. So they took him to the nearest hospital in the hope that his life could be saved, in order that they might interrogate him once the bullet was removed.

I waited for Edith to pause in her story, as she did from time to time, to try to remember each detail in the right order. She had days of the week to assist her now. That Friday night was well remembered. I told her what her mother had said to me about Captain Trevelyan after he was operated on at the hospital.

"Why did your mother put the Captain into an induced coma?" I asked her, but she didn't answer immediately.

"When I think back now, I wonder what would have happened if my mother had simply kept silent and let my father do that terrible deed. Perhaps my father had spoken to her and convinced her that the only solution was to collaborate with the Germans. And yet, I do not think she spoke to him about my discovery, about the fact that Laurent had been tortured. I think she was torn between her husband and her sons and could not accept that he betrayed us all."

Edith knelt down on the promenade and took Gretel's head between her two hands. I sensed what she was thinking about how life goes on relentlessly, whatever actions we take, life still goes on.

"Then Captain Trevelyan arrived in the hospital," she continued. "Onto the very same ward that my mother was working on as a nurse. He was guarded at all times, only the nurses had access to him and the Germans did not realise that my mother was originally from England, or that she spoke English."

Events finally fell into their true order and Edith's story continued more rapidly. She seemed relieved to be telling someone about those terrible events at last.

Trevelyan had very few options available to him, she recounted. His mission was to make contact with the local resistance but his contact was now dead. Whether that was Laurent, or one of the other five members who were executed, he never said, well not until he found out who his English speaking nurse actually was. He had to trust someone and this nurse was the only person he had contact with who spoke English. He was hesitant until she leaned over him and he saw her name on the ID badge.

"Is that a common name?" he asked her. The guards took little notice.

She shook her head.

"We are the only Fourniers in Berck." She whispered, realising that there was more to his question than a simple passing comment.

She stepped back and pulled the curtain around the bed. One of the soldiers thought about questioning her action, but chose not to and the pair found themselves alone.

"Laurent is my contact," he said as quietly as possible.

"Laurent is my son, but he is dead."

Unhesitatingly, he whispered to her the details of his mission. The resistance was to ensure that the local aerodrome, and any aircraft that were based there, had been made inactive before Monday.

"Even knowing this information could get someone killed, Trevelyan told my mother."

Edith paused again and sat back down on to the bench. She repeated the dialogue from the hospital as if she had been there herself.

"What must I do?" Veronique asked.

"Listen," the Captain whispered in her ear and the next words shook her to her soul. "You mustn't let them interrogate me. Kill me if you have to, but they must not find out what I know. It is essential, if the invasion is to succeed, that the airfield is destroyed."

"But," she uttered, "I cannot take your life."

259

"The Gestapo will torture me. I might talk. You must do it, please."

Edith stood up again and said she wanted to walk, suggesting that we head back along the promenade into town. I agreed, but only if she told me what happened next. I knew, of course, that her mother had administered a drug which the hospital used to induce a coma. It was the one they used to sedate highly traumatised accident victims. I knew also that Veronique had told the Germans that the Captain had slipped into a coma.

"My mother returned home late from her shift at the hospital that night. The Germans were insisting to the doctors that something needed to be done to revive the Captain, but the medical staff could give no indication when he might come out of the coma."

Saturday was the busiest day at the bakers, she told me and Edith's father always left Bruno to finish clearing up whilst he joined some of his friends at a bar in the Rue Carnot. When her mother told her about the British airman and what the Captain had said, Edith ran to the shop to tell her brother.

"Bruno understood immediately that the airfield needed to be destroyed, or put out of action, by the end of the following day."

Friday, Saturday, Sunday, I thought to myself. These were the three days Edith had been thinking about earlier.

When Edith returned home from the shop, she met her father coming out of their house.

"Where have you been?" he asked her and she realised immediately that mother had told him everything she had learned from the British airman.

"Where are you going?" Edith asked him.

"To see Bruno."

"I have already told him."

"I still need to go out," he declared and barged passed her, heading off back down the Rue Carnot towards the convent.

Her heart was beating faster and she decided to follow him. He did not go into the bakery but, instead, crossed the road in order that Bruno did not see him. He continued in the direction of the convent, where the Gestapo were now based and turned into the quiet narrow residential street where it was situated. He paused on the corner and looked over his shoulder before heading towards the steps up to the convent door. Through the darkness he could see someone loitering behind him. Edith ducked back into a doorway but could hear his footsteps as he slowly walked back towards her.

She saw her own shadow, cast outward from the doorway, and inched her body back into the entrance, pulling her handbag up to her chest to make the shadow less obvious.

"Edith," her father gasped as he looked into the doorway, not expecting to see her. "What are you doing here?"

"I *know* father," she replied.

His eyes refocused in the darkness of the doorway and he could see the look of fear in her eyes. The three words she had spoken needed no clarification.

"Dieter told you did he?"

"No, I worked it out for myself. Dad, don't do this, please."

"I am saving my family."

"You are destroying our family. Laurent was tortured and murdered by the people you are now helping."

"Nonsense," he shouted "now go home."

He pushed her out of the doorway and stood there for a moment, waiting for her to leave. The handbag was still held to her chest and she felt the heavy object inside it. She reached into the handbag and felt the handle of the gun.

He looked up and down the street to make sure that nobody was around. "Go!" he declared. "I have business to attend to."

Without removing the pistol from inside the bag she pulled the trigger. The blast ripped through the bag and the bullet slammed into her father's chest, knocking him backwards and down on to the ground.

"I looked at him for a moment. He was not moving and a puddle of blood was oozing from beneath his body. I turned and ran back home."

I didn't know what to say to her. Our walk was nearly at an end. We had arrived at the corner of the street where Bruno lived and she continued talking as we stood there.

"What explosives the resistance had hidden away," she said, "were used to destroy the landing strip at the aerodrome and to cause as much damage to the aircraft as they could. The weather delayed the planned invasion, but two days later the allies successfully landed on beaches further down the French coast and the people of Berck were one of the first to be liberated from the German occupation."

In the days that followed, the Germans were too busy, to conduct an investigation into the death of the local baker.

I wanted to ask her so many questions but, in both senses, our journey had ended. There was no more to add. The answers to most of the questions were obvious, like why Edith took holy orders. To punish herself for the crime she had committed, or perhaps to escape the nightmare that was engulfing her, or to simply find peace. I could take my pick, they were all the truth, or one version of it.

Later that week, Sister Marie-Claire returned to the convent in Rome. As far as I know, she never told Bruno about the terrible events of twenty years ago, or even about her involvement in the death of her father. Bruno was her younger brother and she wanted to protect him from the awful truth about his elder brother's torture and the circumstances of their father's death. She did not know whether her mother had told him, but it didn't matter.

Edith placed her hand on my shoulder and said she would leave it to me to judge who should be told about the events of that awful time twenty years ago. The decision would rest with me on who should know the truth regarding the identity of the traitor Saturn. I think perhaps she felt unable to speak ill of her own father and yet felt uncomfortable with concealing the truth.

I nodded and told her that it would be unworthy of us to cover up such a memory. It is important that the truth should never die the mortal death reserved for each of us; otherwise, in some deviant way, the events of that time are lost forever, denied, invalidated in some way, as if they had never occurred, and that would break faith with the truth, make it appear unworthy and make us unworthy through our silence. Truth must never be concealed, truth needs to be spoken in a loud voice, the actual truth, not another version of it.

SURE
UNCERTAINTY

Terrorists are planning an attack in London. But they're not Jihadists – they are British. If caught, they will be publicly executed in the shadow of the building they intended to blow up.

This is a story of secrets, family secrets and others too, no less personal or deserving of concealment. Some guarded through this life, sheltered like skeletons in cupboards and taken to the grave; others shared by the feeble and faint-hearted and through that sharing put to the test, then exposed - just like the individuals who carried them.

This is Shakespeare and Marlowe but not as writers. Forget what you are certain about or what you are sure you know - this is the story of the gunpowder plot. This is the story of Sure Uncertainty.

Follow the author on Twitter
Peter Larner@OpusWriter